THE MONSTERS
AND OTHER SCIENCE FICTION TALES

ROBERT SHECKLEY

PUBLISHED BY BROWNSTONE BOOKS

THE MONSTERS
AND OTHER SCIENCE FICTION TALES

CONTENTS

THE MONSTERS

CORDOVIR AND HUM STOOD on the rocky mountaintop, watching the new thing happen. Both felt rather good about it. It was undoubtedly the newest thing that had happened for some time.

"By the way the sunlight glints from it," Hum said, "I'd say it is made of metal."

"I'll accept that," Cordovir said. "But what holds it up in the air?"

They both stared intently down to the valley where the new thing was happening. A pointed object was hovering over the ground. From one end of it poured a substance resembling fire.

"It's balancing on the fire," Hum said. "That should be apparent even to your old eyes."

Cordovir lifted himself higher on his thick tail, to get a better look. The object settled to the ground and the fire stopped.

"Shall we go down and have a closer look?" Hum asked.

"All right. I think we have time—wait! What day is this?"

Hum calculated silently, then said, "The fifth day of Luggat."

"Damn," Cordovir said. "I have to go home and kill my wife."

1

"It's a few hours before sunset," Hum said. "I think you have time to do both."

Cordovir wasn't sure. "I'd hate to be late."

"Well, then. You know how fast I am," Hum said. "If it gets late, I'll hurry back and kill her myself. How about that?"

"That's very decent of you." Cordovir thanked the younger man and together they slithered down the steep mountainside.

In front of the metal object both men halted and stood up on their tails.

"Rather bigger than I thought," Cordovir said, measuring the metal object with his eye. He estimated that it was slightly longer than their village, and almost half as wide. They crawled a circle around it, observing that the metal was tooled, presumably by human tentacles.

In the distance the smaller sun had set.

"I think we had better get back," Cordovir said, noting the cessation of light.

"*I* still have plenty of time." Hum flexed his muscles complacently.

"Yes, but a man likes to kill his own wife."

"As you wish." They started off to the village at a brisk pace.

In his house, Cordovir's wife was finishing supper. She had her back to the door, as etiquette required. Cordovir killed her with a single flying slash of his tail, dragged her body outside, and sat down to eat.

After meal and meditation he went to the Gathering. Hum, with the impatience of youth, was already there, telling of the metal object. He probably bolted his supper, Cordovir thought with mild distaste.

After the youngster had finished, Cordovir gave his own observations. The only thing he added to Hum's account was an idea: that the metal object might contain intelligent beings.

"What makes you think so?" Mishill, another elder, asked.

"The fact that there was fire from the object as it came down," Cordovir said, "joined to the fact that the fire stopped after the object was on the ground. Some being, I contend, was responsible for turning it off."

"Not necessarily," Mishill said. The village men talked about it late into the night. Then they broke up the meeting, buried the various murdered wives, and went to their homes.

Lying in the darkness, Cordovir discovered that he hadn't made up his mind as yet about the new thing. Presuming it contained intelligent beings, would they be moral? Would they have a sense of right and wrong? Cordovir doubted it, and went to sleep.

The next morning every male in the village went to the metal object. This was proper, since the functions of males were to examine new things and to limit the female population. They formed a circle around it, speculating on what might be inside.

"I believe they will be human beings," Hum's elder brother Esktel said. Cordovir shook his entire body in disagreement.

"Monsters, more likely," he said. "If you take in account—"

"Not necessarily," Esktel said. "Consider the logic of our physical development. A single focusing eye—"

"But in the great Òutside," Cordovir said, "there may be many strange races, most of them non-human. In the infinitude—"

"Still," Esktel put in, "the logic of our—"

"As I was saying," Cordovir went on, "the chance is infinitesimal that they would resemble us. Their vehicle, for example. Would we build—"

"But on strictly logical grounds," Esktel said, "you can see—"

That was the third time Cordovir had been interrupted. With a single movement of his tail he smashed Esktel against the metal object. Esktel fell to the ground, dead.

"I have often considered my brother a boor," Hum said. "What were you saying?"

But Cordovir was interrupted again. A piece of metal set in the greater piece of metal squeaked, turned and lifted, and a creature came out.

Cordovir saw at once that he had been right. The thing that crawled out of the hole was twin-tailed. It was covered to its top with something partially metal and partially hide. And its color! Cordovir shuddered.

The thing was the color of wet, flayed flesh.

All the villagers had backed away, waiting to see what the thing would do. At first it didn't do anything. It stood on the metal surface, and a bulbous object that topped its body moved from side to side. But there were no accompanying body movements to give the gesture meaning. Finally, the thing raised both tentacles and made noises.

"Do you think it's trying to communicate?" Mishill asked softly.

Three more creatures appeared in the metal hole, carrying metal sticks in their tentacles. The things made noises at each other.

"They are decidedly not human," Cordovir said firmly. "The next question is, are they moral beings?" One of the things crawled down the metal side and stood on the ground. The rest pointed their metal sticks at the ground. It seemed to be some sort of religious ceremony.

"Could anything so hideous be moral?" Cordovir asked, his hide twitching with distaste. Upon closer inspection, the creatures were more horrible than could be dreamed. The bulbous object on their bodies just might be a head, Cordovir decided, even though it was unlike any head he had ever seen. But in the middle of that head! Instead of a smooth, characterful surface was a raised ridge. Two round indentures were on either side of it, and two more knobs on either side of that. And in the lower half of the head—if such it was—a pale, reddish slash ran across. Cordovir supposed this might be considered a mouth, with some stretching of the imagination.

Nor was this all, Cordovir observed. The things were so constructed as to show the presence of bone! When they moved their limbs, it wasn't a smooth, flowing gesture, the fluid motion of human beings. Rather, it was the jerky snap of a tree limb.

"God above," Gilrig, an intermediate-age male gasped. "We should kill them and put them out of their misery!" Other men seemed to feel the same way, and the villagers flowed forward.

"Wait!" one of the youngsters shouted. "Let's communicate with them, if such is possible. They might still be moral beings. The Outside is wide, remember, and anything is possible."

Cordovir argued for immediate extermination, but the villagers stopped and discussed it among themselves. Hum, with characteristic bravado, flowed up to the thing on the ground.

"Hello," Hum said.

The thing said something.

"I can't understand it," Hum said, and started to crawl back. The creature waved its jointed tentacles—if they were tentacles—and motioned at one of the suns. He made a sound.

"Yes, it is warm, isn't it?" Hum said cheerfully.

The creature pointed at the ground, and made another sound.

"We haven't had especially good crops this year," Hum said conversationally.

The creature pointed at itself and made a sound.

"I agree," Hum said. "You're as ugly as sin."

Presently the villagers grew hungry and crawled back to the village. Hum stayed and listened to the things making noises at him, and Cordovir waited nervously for Hum.

"You know," Hum said, after he rejoined Cordovir, "I think they want to learn our language. Or want me to learn theirs."

"Don't do it," Cordovir said, glimpsing the misty edge of a great evil.

"I believe I will," Hum murmured. Together they climbed the cliffs back to the village.

That afternoon Cordovir went to the surplus female pen and formally asked a young woman if she would reign in his house for twenty-five days. Naturally, the woman accepted gratefully.

On the way home, Cordovir met Hum, going to the pen.

"Just killed my wife," Hum said, superfluously, since why else would he be going to the surplus female stock?

"Are you going back to the creatures tomorrow?" Cordovir asked.

"I might," Hum answered, "if nothing new presents itself."

"The thing to find out is if they are moral beings or monsters."

"Right," Hum said, and slithered on.

There was a Gathering that evening, after supper. All the villagers agreed that the things were non-human. Cordovir argued strenuously that their very appearance belied any possibility of humanity. Nothing so hideous could have moral standards, a sense of right and wrong, and above all, a notion of truth.

The young men didn't agree, probably because there had been a dearth of new things recently. They pointed out that the metal object was obviously a product of intelligence. Intelligence axiomatically means standards of differentiation. Differentiation implies right and wrong.

It was a delicious argument. Olgolel contradicted Arast and was killed by him. Mavrt, in an unusual fit of anger for so placid an individual, killed the three Holian brothers and was himself killed by Hum, who was feeling pettish. Even the surplus females could be heard arguing about it, in their pen in a corner of the village.

Weary and happy, the villagers went to sleep.

The next few weeks saw no end of the argument. Life went on much as usual, though. The women went out in the morning, gathered food, prepared it, and laid eggs. The eggs were taken to the surplus females to be hatched. As usual, about eight females were hatched to every male. On the twenty-fifth day of each marriage, or a little earlier, each man killed his woman and took another.

The males went down to the ship to listen to Hum learning the language; then, when that grew boring, they returned to their customary wandering through hills and forests, looking for new things.

The alien monsters stayed close to their ship, coming out only when Hum was there.

Twenty-four days after the arrival of the non-humans, Hum announced that he could communicate with them, after a fashion.

"They say they come from far away," Hum told the village that evening. "They say that they are bisexual, like us, and that they are humans, like us. They say there are reasons for their different appearance, but I couldn't understand that part of it."

"If we accept them as humans," Mishill said, "then everything they say is true."

The rest of the villagers shook in agreement.

"They say that they don't want to disturb our life, but would be very interested in observing it. They want to come to the village and look around."

"I see no reason why not," one of the younger men said.

"No!" Cordovir shouted. "You are letting in evil. These monsters are insidious. I believe that they are capable of —telling an untruth!" The other elders agreed, but when pressed, Cordovir had no proof to back up this vicious accusation.

"After all," Sil pointed out, "just because they look like monsters, you can't take it for granted that they think like monsters as well."

"I can," Cordovir said, but he was outvoted.

Hum went on. "They have offered me—or us, I'm not sure which, various metal objects which they say will do various things. I ignored this breach of etiquette, since I considered they didn't know any better."

Cordovir nodded. The youngster was growing up. He was showing, at long last, that he had some manners.

"They want to come to the village tomorrow."

"No!" Cordovir shouted, but the vote was against him.

"Oh, by the way," Hum said, as the meeting was breaking up. "They have several females among them. The ones with the very red mouths are females. It will be interesting to see how the males kill them. Tomorrow is the twenty-fifth day since they came."

The next day the things came to the village, crawling slowly and laboriously over the cliffs. The villagers were able to observe the extreme brittleness of their limbs, the terrible awkwardness of their motions.

"No beauty whatsoever," Cordovir muttered. "And they all look alike."

In the village the things acted without any decency. They crawled into huts and out of huts. They jabbered at the surplus female pen. They picked up eggs and examined them. They peered at the villagers through black things and shiny things.

In midafternoon, Rantan, an elder, decided it was about time he killed his woman. So he pushed the thing who was examining his hut aside and smashed his female to death.

Instantly, two of the things started jabbering at each other, hurrying out of the hut.

One had the red mouth of a female.

"He must have remembered it was time to kill his own woman," Hum observed. The villagers waited, but nothing happened.

"Perhaps," Rantan said, "perhaps he would like someone to kill her for him. It might be the custom of their land."

Without further ado Rantan slashed down the female with his tail.

The male creature made a terrible noise and pointed a metal stick at Rantan. Rantan collapsed, dead.

"That's odd," Mishill said. "I wonder if that denotes disapproval?"

The things from the metal object—eight of them—were in a tight little circle. One was holding the dead female, and the rest were pointing the metal sticks on all sides. Hum went up and asked them what was wrong.

"I don't understand," Hum said, after he spoke with them. "They used words I haven't learned. But I gather that their emotion is one of reproach."

The monsters were backing away. Another villager, deciding it was about time, killed his wife who was standing in a doorway. The group of monsters stopped and jabbered at each other. Then they motioned to Hum.

Hum's body motion was incredulous after he had talked with them.

"If I understood right," Hum said, "They are ordering us not to kill any more of our women!"

"What!" Cordovir and a dozen others shouted.

"I'll ask them again." Hum went back into conference with the monsters who were waving metal sticks in their tentacles.

"That's right," Hum said. Without further preamble

he flipped his tail, throwing one of the monsters across the village square. Immediately the others began to point their sticks while retreating rapidly.

After they were gone, the villagers found that seventeen males were dead. Hum, for some reason, had been missed.

"Now will you believe me!" Cordovir shouted. "The creatures told *a deliberate untruth!* They said they wouldn't molest us and then they proceed to kill seventeen of us! Not only an amoral act—but a *concerted death effort!*"

It was almost past human understanding.

"A deliberate untruth!" Cordovir shouted the blasphemy, sick with loathing. Men rarely discussed the possibility of anyone telling an untruth.

The villagers were beside themselves with anger and revulsion, once they realized the full concept of an *untruthful* creature. And, added to that was the monsters' concerted death effort!

It was like the most horrible nightmare come true. Suddenly it became apparent that these creatures didn't kill females. Undoubtedly they allowed them to spawn unhampered. The thought of that was enough to make a strong man retch.

The surplus females broke out of their pens and, joined by the wives, demanded to know what was happening. When they were told, they were twice as indignant as the men, such being the nature of women.

"Kill them!" the surplus females roared. "Don't let them change our ways. Don't let them introduce immorality!"

"It's true," Hum said sadly. "I should have guessed it."

"They must be killed at once!" a female shouted. Being surplus, she had no name at present, but she made up for that in blazing personality.

"We women desire only to live moral, decent lives, hatching eggs in the pen until our time of marriage comes. And then twenty-five ecstatic days! How could we desire more? These monsters will destroy our way of life. They will make us as terrible as they!"

"Now do you understand?" Cordovir screamed at the men. "I warned you, I presented it to you, and you ignored me! Young men must listen to old men in time of crisis!" In his rage he killed two youngsters with a blow of his tail. The villagers applauded.

"Drive them out," Cordovir shouted. "Before they corrupt us!"

All the females rushed off to kill the monsters.

"They have death-sticks," Hum observed. "Do the females know?"

"I don't believe so," Cordovir said. He was completely calm now. "You'd better go and tell them."

"I'm tired," Hum said sulkily. "I've been translating. Why don't you go?"

"Oh, let's both go," Cordovir said, bored with the youngster's adolescent moodiness. Accompanied by half the villagers they hurried off after the females.

They overtook them on the edge of the cliff that overlooked the object. Hum explained the death-sticks while Cordovir considered the problem.

"Roll stones on them," he told the females. "Perhaps you can break the metal of the object."

The females started rolling stones down the cliffs with great energy. Some bounced off the metal of the object. Immediately, lines of red fire came from the object and females were killed. The ground shook.

"Let's move back," Cordovir said. "The females have it well in hand, and this shaky ground makes me giddy."

Together with the rest of the males they moved to a safe distance and watched the action.

Women were dying right and left, but they were reinforced by women of other villages who had heard of the menace. They were fighting for their homes now, their rights, and they were fiercer than a man could ever be. The object was throwing fire all over the cliff, but the fire helped dislodge more stones which rained down on the thing. Finally, big fires came out of one end of the metal object.

A landslide started, and the object got into the air just in time. It barely missed a mountain; then it climbed steadily, until it was a little black speck against the larger sun. And then it was gone.

That evening, it was discovered that 53 females had been killed. This was fortunate since it helped keep down the surplus female population. The problem would become even more acute now, since seventeen males were gone in a single lump.

Cordovir was feeling exceedingly proud of himself. His wife had been gloriously killed in the fighting, but he took another at once.

"We had better kill our wives sooner than every twenty-five days for a while," he said at the evening Gathering. "Just until things get back to normal."

The surviving females, back in the pen, heard him and applauded wildly.

"I wonder where the things have gone," Hum said, offering the question to the Gathering.

"Probably away to enslave some defenseless race," Cordovir said.

"Not necessarily," Mishill put in and the evening argument was on.

COST
OF LIVING

CARRIN DECIDED that he could trace his present mood to Miller's suicide last week. But the knowledge didn't help him get rid of the vague, formless fears in the back of his mind. It was foolish. Miller's suicide didn't concern him.

But why had that fat, jovial man killed himself? Miller had had everything to live for—wife, kids, good job, and all the marvelous luxuries of the age. Why had he done it?

"Good morning, dear," Carrin's wife said as he sat down at the breakfast table.

"Morning, honey. Morning, Billy."

His son grunted something.

You just couldn't tell about people, Carrin decided, and dialed his breakfast. The meal was gracefully prepared and served by the new Avignon Electric Auto-cook.

His mood persisted, annoyingly enough since Carrin wanted to be in top form this morning. It was his day off, and the Avignon Electric finance man was coming. This was an important day.

He walked to the door with his son.

"Have a good day, Billy."

His son nodded, shifted his books and started to school without answering. Carrin wondered if something was bothering him, too. He hoped not. One worrier in the family was plenty.

"See you later, honey." He kissed his wife as she left to go shopping.

At any rate, he thought, watching her go down the walk, she's happy. He wondered how much she'd spend at the A. E. store.

Checking his watch, he found that he had half an hour before the A. E. finance man was due. The best way to get rid of a bad mood was to drown it, he told himself, and headed for the shower.

The shower room was a glittering plastic wonder, and the sheer luxury of it eased Carrin's mind. He threw his clothes into the A. E. automatic Kleen-presser, and adjusted the shower spray to a notch above "brisk." The five-degrees-above-skin-temperature water beat against his thin white body. Delightful! And then a relaxing rub-dry in the A. E. Auto-towel.

Wonderful, he thought, as the towel stretched and kneaded his stringy muscles. And it should be wonderful, he reminded himself. The A. E. Auto-towel with shaving attachments had cost three hundred and thirteen dollars, plus tax.

But worth every penny of it, he decided, as the A. E. shaver came out of a corner and whisked off his rudimentary stubble. After all, what good was life if you couldn't enjoy the luxuries?

His skin tingled when he switched off the Auto-towel. He should have been feeling wonderful, but he wasn't. Miller's suicide kept nagging at his mind, destroying the peace of his day off.

Was there anything else bothering him? Certainly there was nothing wrong with the house. His papers were in order for the finance man.

"Have I forgotten something?" he asked out loud.

"The Avignon Electric finance man will be here in fifteen minutes," his A. E. bathroom Wall-reminder whispered.

"I know that. Is there anything else?"

The Wall-reminder reeled off its memorized data—a vast amount of minutiae about watering the lawn, having the Jet-lash checked, buying lamb chops for Monday, and the like. Things he still hadn't found time for.

"All right, that's enough." He allowed the A. E. Auto-dresser to dress him, skillfully draping a new selection of fabrics over his bony frame. A whiff of fashionable masculine perfume finished him and he went into the living room, threading his way between the appliances that lined the walls.

A quick inspection of the dials on the wall assured him that the house was in order. The breakfast dishes had been sanitized and stacked, the house had been cleaned, dusted, polished, his wife's garments had been hung up, his son's model rocket ships had been put back in the closet.

Stop worrying, you hypochondriac, he told himself angrily.

The door announced, "Mr. Pathis from Avignon Finance is here."

Carrin started to tell the door to open, when he noticed the Automatic Bartender.

Good God, why hadn't he thought of it!

The Automatic Bartender was manufactured by Castile Motors. He had bought it in a weak moment. A. E. wouldn't think very highly of that, since they sold their own brand.

He wheeled the bartender into the kitchen, and told the door to open.

"A very good day to you, sir," Mr. Pathis said.

Pathis was a tall, imposing man, dressed in a conservative tweed drape. His eyes had the crinkled corners of a man who laughs frequently. He beamed broadly and shook Carrin's hand, looking around the crowded living room.

"A beautiful place you have here, sir. Beautiful! As a matter of fact, I don't think I'll be overstepping the company's code to inform you that yours is the nicest interior in this section."

Carrin felt a sudden glow of pride at that, thinking of the rows of identical houses, on this block and the next, and the one after that.

"Now, then, is everything functioning properly?" Mr. Pathis asked, setting his briefcase on a chair. "Everything in order?"

"Oh, yes," Carrin said enthusiastically. "Avignon Electric never goes out of whack."

"The phono all right? Changes records for the full seventeen hours?"

"It certainly does," Carrin said. He hadn't had a chance

to try out the phono, but it was a beautiful piece of furniture.

"The Solido-projector all right? Enjoying the programs?"

"Absolutely perfect reception." He had watched a program just last month, and it had been startlingly lifelike.

"How about the kitchen? Auto-cook in order? Recipe-master still knocking 'em out?"

"Marvelous stuff. Simply marvelous."

Mr. Pathis went on to inquire about his refrigerator, his vacuum cleaner, his car, his helicopter, his subterranean swimming pool, and the hundreds of other items Carrin had bought from Avignon Electric.

"Everything is swell," Carrin said, a trifle untruthfully since he hadn't unpacked every item yet. "Just wonderful."

"I'm so glad," Mr. Pathis said, leaning back with a sigh of relief. "You have no idea how hard we try to satisfy our customers. If a product isn't right, back it comes, no questions asked. We believe in pleasing our customers."

"I certainly appreciate it, Mr. Pathis."

Carrin hoped the A. E. man wouldn't ask to see the kitchen. He visualized the Castile Motors Bartender in there, like a porcupine in a dog show.

"I'm proud to say that most of the people in this neighborhood buy from us," Mr. Pathis was saying. "We're a solid firm."

"Was Mr. Miller a customer of yours?" Carrin asked.

"That fellow who killed himself?" Pathis frowned briefly. "He was, as a matter of fact. That amazed me, sir, absolutely amazed me. Why, just last month the fellow bought a brand-new Jet-lash from me, capable of doing three hundred and fifty miles an hour on a straightaway. He was as happy as a kid over it, and then to go and do a thing like that! Of course, the Jet-lash brought up his debt a little."

"Of course."

"But what did that matter? He had every luxury in the world. And then he went and hung himself."

"Hung himself?"

"Yes," Pathis said, the frown coming back. "Every modern convenience in his house, and he hung himself with a piece of rope. Probably unbalanced for a long time."

The frown slid off his face, and the customary smile replaced it. "But enough of that! Let's talk about you."

The smile widened as Pathis opened his briefcase. "Now, then, your account. You owe us two hundred and three thousand dollars and twenty-nine cents, Mr. Carrin, as of your last purchase. Right?"

"Right," Carrin said, remembering the amount from his own papers. "Here's my installment."

He handed Pathis an envelope, which the man checked and put in his pocket.

"Fine. Now you know, Mr. Carrin, that you won't live long enough to pay us the full two hundred thousand, don't you?"

"No, I don't suppose I will," Carrin said soberly.

He was only thirty-nine, with a full hundred years of life before him, thanks to the marvels of medical science. But at a salary of three thousand a year, he still couldn't pay it all off and have enough to support a family on at the same time.

"Of course, we would not want to deprive you of necessities. To say nothing of the terrific items that are coming out next year. Things you wouldn't want to miss, sir!"

Mr. Carrin nodded. Certainly he wanted new items.

"Well, suppose we make the customary arrangement. If you will just sign over your son's earnings for the first thirty years of his adult life, we can easily arrange credit for you."

Mr. Pathis whipped the papers out of his briefcase and spread them in front of Carrin.

"If you'll just sign here, sir."

"Well," Carrin said, "I'm not sure. I'd like to give the boy a start in life, not saddle him with—"

"But my dear sir," Pathis interposed, "this is for your son as well. He lives here, doesn't he? He has a right to enjoy the luxuries, the marvels of science."

"Sure," Carrin said. "Only—"

"Why, sir, today the average man is living like a king. A hundred years ago the richest man in the world couldn't buy what any ordinary citizen possesses at present. You mustn't look upon it as a debt. It's an investment."

"That's true," Carrin said dubiously.

He thought about his son and his rocket ship models, his star charts, his maps. Would it be right? he asked himself.

"What's wrong?" Pathis asked cheerfully.

"Well, I was just wondering," Carrin said. "Signing over my son's earnings—you don't think I'm getting in a little too deep, do you?"

"Too deep? My dear sir!" Pathis exploded into laughter. "Do you know Mellon down the block? Well, don't say I said it, but he's already mortgaged his grandchildren's salary for their full life-expectancy! And he doesn't have half the goods he's made up his mind to own! We'll work out something for him. Service to the customer is our job and we know it well."

Carrin wavered visibly.

"And after you're gone, sir, they'll all belong to your son."

That was true, Carrin thought. His son would have all the marvelous things that filled the house. And after all, it was only thirty years out of a life expectancy of a hundred and fifty.

He signed with a flourish.

"Excellent!" Pathis said. "And by the way, has your home got an A. E. Master-operator?"

It hadn't. Pathis explained that a Master-operator was

new this year, a stupendous advance in scientific engineering. It was designed to take over all the functions of housecleaning and cooking, without its owner having to lift a finger.

"Instead of running around all day, pushing half a dozen different buttons, with the Master-operator all you have to do is push *one!* A remarkable achievement!"

Since it was only five hundred and thirty-five dollars, Carrin signed for one, having it added to his son's debt.

Right's right, he thought, walking Pathis to the door. This house will be Billy's some day. His and his wife's. They certainly will want everything up-to-date.

Just one button, he thought. That *would* be a time-saver!

After Pathis left, Carrin sat back in an adjustable chair and turned on the solido. After twisting the Ezi-dial, he discovered that there was nothing he wanted to see. He tilted back the chair and took a nap.

The something on his mind was still bothering him.

"Hello, darling!" He awoke to find his wife was home. She kissed him on the ear. "Look."

She had bought an A. E. Sexitizer-negligee. He was pleasantly surprised that that was all she had bought. Usually, Leela returned from shopping laden down.

"It's lovely," he said.

She bent over for a kiss, then giggled—a habit he knew she had picked up from the latest popular solido star. He wished she hadn't.

"Going to dial supper," she said, and went to the kitchen. Carrin smiled, thinking that soon she would be able to dial the meals without moving out of the living room. He settled back in his chair, and his son walked in.

"How's it going, Son?" he asked heartily.

"All right," Billy answered listlessly.

"What'sa matter, Son?" The boy stared at his feet, not answering. "Come on, tell Dad what's the trouble."

Billy sat down on a packing case and put his chin in his hands. He looked thoughtfully at his father.

"Dad, could I be a Master Repairman if I wanted to be?"

Mr. Carrin smiled at the question. Billy alternated between wanting to be a Master Repairman and a rocket pilot. The repairmen were the elite. It was their job to fix the automatic repair machines. The repair machines could fix just about anything, but you couldn't have a machine fix the machine that fixed the machine. That was where the Master Repairmen came in.

But it was a highly competitive field and only a very few of the best brains were able to get their degrees. And, although the boy was bright, he didn't seem to have an engineering bent.

"It's possible, Son. Anything is possible."

"But is it possible for me?"

"I don't know," Carrin answered, as honestly as he could.

"Well, I don't want to be a Master Repairman anyway," the boy said, seeing that the answer was no. "I want to be a space pilot."

"A space pilot, Billy?" Leela asked, coming in to the room. "But there aren't any."

"Yes, there are," Billy argued. "We were told in school that the government is going to send some men to Mars."

"They've been saying that for a hundred years," Carrin said, "and they still haven't gotten around to doing it."

"They will this time."

"Why would you want to go to Mars?" Leela asked, winking at Carrin. "There are no pretty girls on Mars."

"I'm not interested in girls. I just want to go to Mars."

"You wouldn't like it, honey." Leela said. "It's a nasty old place with no air."

"It's got some air. I'd like to go there," the boy insisted sullenly. "I don't like it here."

"What's that?" Carrin asked, sitting up straight. "Is there anything you haven't got? Anything you want?"

"No, sir. I've got everything I want." Whenever his son called him 'sir,' Carrin knew that something was wrong.

"Look, Son, when I was your age I wanted to go to Mars, too. I wanted to do romantic things. I even wanted to be a Master Repairman."

"Then why didn't you?"

"Well, I grew up. I realized that there were more important things. First I had to pay off the debt my father had left me, and then I met your mother—"

Leela giggled.

"—and I wanted a home of my own. It'll be the same with you. You'll pay off your debt and get married, the same as the rest of us."

Billy was silent for a while. Then he brushed his dark hair—straight, like his father's—back from his forehead and wet his lips.

"How come I have debts, sir?"

Carrin explained carefully. About the things a family needed for civilized living, and the cost of those items. How they had to be paid. How it was customary for a son to take on a part of his parent's debt, when he came of age.

Billy's silence annoyed him. It was almost as if the boy were reproaching him. After he had slaved for years to give the ungrateful whelp every luxury!

"Son," he said harshly, "have you studied history in school? Good. Then you know how it was in the past. Wars. How would you like to get blown up in a war?"

The boy didn't answer.

"Or how would you like to break your back for eight hours a day, doing work a machine should handle? Or be hungry all the time? Or cold, with the rain beating down on you, and no place to sleep?"

He paused for a response, got none and went on. "You

live in the most fortunate age mankind has ever known. You are surrounded by every wonder of art and science. The finest music, the greatest books and art, all at your fingertips. All you have to do is push a button." He shifted to a kindlier tone. "Well, what are you thinking?"

"I was just wondering how I could go to Mars," the boy said. "With the debt, I mean. I don't suppose I could get away from that."

"Of course not."

"Unless I stowed away on a rocket."

"But you wouldn't do that."

"No, of course not," the boy said, but his tone lacked conviction.

"You'll stay here and marry a very nice girl," Leela told him.

"Sure I will," Billy said. "Sure." He grinned suddenly. "I didn't mean any of that stuff about going to Mars. I really didn't."

"I'm glad of that," Leela answered.

"Just forget I mentioned it," Billy said, smiling stiffly. He stood up and raced upstairs.

"Probably gone to play with his rockets," Leela said. "He's such a little devil."

The Carrins ate a quiet supper, and then it was time for Mr. Carrin to go to work. He was on night shift this month. He kissed his wife good-by, climbed into his Jetlash and roared to the factory. The automatic gates recognized him and opened. He parked and walked in.

Automatic lathes, automatic presses—everything was automatic. The factory was huge and bright, and the machines hummed softly to themselves, doing their job and doing it well.

Carrin walked to the end of the automatic washing machine assembly line, to relieve the man there.

"Everything all right?" he asked.

"Sure," the man said. "Haven't had a bad one all year."

These new models here have built-in voices. They don't light up like the old ones."

Carrin sat down where the man had sat and waited for the first washing machine to come through. His job was the soul of simplicity. He just sat there and the machines went by him. He pressed a button on them and found out if they were all right. They always were. After passing him, the washing machines went to the packaging section.

The first one slid by on the long slide of rollers. He pressed the starting button on the side.

"Ready for the wash," the washing machine said.

Carrin pressed the release and let it go by.

That boy of his, Carrin thought. Would he grow up and face his responsibilities? Would he mature and take his place in society? Carrin doubted it. The boy was a born rebel. If anyone got to Mars, it would be his kid.

But the thought didn't especially disturb him.

"Ready for the wash." Another machine went by.

Carrin remembered something about Miller. The jovial man had always been talking about the planets, always kidding about going off somewhere and roughing it. He hadn't, though. He had committed suicide.

"Ready for the wash."

Carrin had eight hours in front of him, and he loosened his belt to prepare for it. Eight hours of pushing buttons and listening to a machine announce its readiness.

"Ready for the wash."

He pressed the release.

"Ready for the wash."

Carrin's mind strayed from the job, which didn't need much attention in any case. He realized now what had been bothering him.

He didn't enjoy pushing buttons.

THE
ALTAR

WITH A SPRIGHTLY GAIT, Mr. Slater walked down Maple Street toward the station. There was a little bounce to his step this morning, and a smile on his clean-shaven substantial face. It was such a glorious spring morning!

Mr. Slater hummed a tune to himself, glad of the seven block walk to the railroad station. Although the distance had been a bother all winter, weather like this made up for it. It was a pleasure to be alive, a joy to be commuting.

Just then he was stopped by a man in a light blue topcoat.

"Pardon me, sir," the man said. "Could you direct me to the Altar of Baz-Matain?"

Mr. Slater, still full of the beauties of spring, tried to think. "Baz-Matain? I don't think—the *Altar* of Baz-Matain, you say?"

"That's right," the stranger said, with an apologetic little smile. He was unusually tall, and he had a dark, thin face. Mr. Slater decided it was a foreign-looking face.

"Terribly sorry," Mr. Slater said, after a moment's thought. "I don't believe I ever heard of it."

"Thanks anyhow," the dark man said, nodded pleasantly and walked off toward the center of town. Mr. Slater continued to the station.

After the conductor punched his ticket, Mr. Slater thought of the incident. *Baz-Matain,* he repeated to himself as the train sped through the misty, ragged fields of New Jersey. *Baz-Matain.* Mr. Slater decided that the foreign-looking man must have been mistaken. North Am-

24

brose, New Jersey, was a small town; small enough for a
resident to know every street in it, every house or store.
Especially a resident of almost twenty years standing, like
Mr. Slater.

Halfway through the office day, Mr. Slater found himself tapping a pencil against the glass top of his desk,
thinking of the man in the light blue topcoat. A foreign-
looking fellow was an oddity in North Ambrose, a quiet,
refined, settled suburb. The North Ambrose men wore
good business suits and carried lean brown suitcases; some
were fat and some were thin, but anyone in North Ambrose might have been taken for anyone else's brother.

Mr. Slater didn't think of it any more. He finished his
day, took the tube to Hoboken, the train to North Ambrose, and finally started the walk to his house.

On the way he passed the man again.

"I found it," the stranger said. "It wasn't easy, but I
found it."

"Where was it?" Mr. Slater asked, stopping.

"Right beside the Temple of Dark Mysteries of Isis,"
the stranger said. "Stupid of me. I should have asked for
that in the first place. I knew it was here, but it never
occurred to me—"

"The temple of what?" Mr. Slater asked.

"Dark Mysteries of Isis," the dark man said. "Not com-
petitors, really. Seers and warlocks, fertility cycles and the
like. Never come near *our* province."

"I see," Mr. Slater said, looking at the stranger closely
in the early spring twilight. "The reason I asked, I've
lived in this town a number of years, and I don't believe
I ever heard—"

"Say!" the man exclaimed, glancing at his watch.
"Didn't realize how late it was! I'll be holding up the
ceremony if I don't hurry!" And with a friendly wave of
his hand, he hurried off.

Mr. Slater walked slowly home, thinking. *Altar of Baz-*

Matain. Dark Mysteries of Isis. They sounded like cults. Could there be such places in his town? It seemed impossible. No one would rent to people like that.

After supper, Mr. Slater consulted the telephone book. But there was no listing for Baz-Matain, or for The Temple of Dark Mysteries of Isis. Information wasn't able to supply them either.

"Odd," he mused. Later, he told his wife about the two meetings with the foreign man.

"Well," she said, pulling her house robe closer around her, "no one's going to start any cults in this town. The Better Business Bureau wouldn't allow it. To say nothing of the Woman's Club, or the P.T.A."

Mr. Slater agreed. The stranger must have had the wrong town. Perhaps the cults were in South Ambrose, a neighboring town with several bars and a movie house, and a distinctly undesirable element in its population.

The next morning was Friday. Mr. Slater looked for the stranger, but all he saw were his homogeneous fellow commuters. It was the same on the way back. Evidently the fellow had visited the Altar and left. Or he had taken up duties there at hours which didn't coincide with Mr. Slater's commuting hours.

Monday morning Mr. Slater left his house a few minutes late and was hurrying to catch his train. Ahead he saw the blue topcoat.

"Hello there," Mr. Slater called.

"Why hello!" the dark man said, his thin face breaking into a smile. "I was wondering when we would bump into each other again."

"So was I," Mr. Slater said, slowing his pace. The stranger was strolling along evidently enjoying the magnificent weather. Mr. Slater knew that he was going to miss his train.

"And how are things at the Altar?" Mr. Slater asked.

"So-so," the man said, his hands clasped behind his

back. "To tell you the truth, we're having a bit of trouble."

"Oh?" Mr. Slater asked.

"Yes," the dark man said, his face stern. "Old Atherhotep, the mayor, is threatening to revoke our license in North Ambrose. Says we aren't fulfilling our charter. But I ask you, how can we? What with the Dionysus-Africanus set across the street grabbing everyone likely, and the Papa Legba-Damballa combine two doors down, taking even the unlikely ones—well, what can you do?"

"It doesn't sound too good," Mr. Slater agreed.

"That's not all," the stranger said. "Our high priest is threatening to leave if we don't get some action. He's a seventh degree adept, and Brahma alone knows where we'd get another."

"Mmm," Mr. Slater murmured.

"That's what *I'm* here for, though," the stranger said. "If they're going to use sharp business practices, I'll go them one better. I'm the new business manager, you know."

"Oh?" Mr. Slater said, surprised. "Are you reorganizing?"

"In a way," the stranger told him. "You see, its like this—" Just then a short, plump man hurried up and seized the dark man by the sleeve of the blue topcoat.

"Elor," he panted. "I miscalculated the date. It's *this* Monday! Today, not next week!"

"Damn," the dark man said succinctly. "You'll have to excuse me," he said to Mr. Slater. "This is rather urgent." He hurried away with the short man.

Mr. Slater was half an hour late for work that morning, but he didn't care. It was all pretty obvious, he thought, sitting at his desk. A group of cults was springing up in North Ambrose, vying for congregations. And the mayor, instead of getting rid of them, was doing nothing. Perhaps he was even taking bribes!

Mr. Slater tapped his pencil against his glass topped desk. How was it possible? Nothing could be hidden in North Ambrose. It was such a little town. Mr. Slater knew a good percentage of the inhabitants by their first names. How could something like this go on unnoticed?

Angrily, he reached for the telephone.

Information was unable to supply him with the numbers of Dionysus Africanus, Papa Legba or Damballa. The mayor of North Ambrose, he was informed, was not Atherhotep, but a man named Miller. Mr. Slater telephoned him.

The conversation was far from satisfying. The mayor insisted that he knew every business in the town, every church, every lodge. And if there were any cults—which there weren't—he would know of them too.

"You have been deluded, my good man," Mayor Miller said, a little too pompously to suit Mr. Slater. "There are no people by those names in this town, no such organizations. We would never allow them in."

Mr. Slater thought this over carefully on the way home. As he stepped off the train platform he saw Elor, hurrying across Oak Street with short, rapid steps.

Elor stopped when Mr. Slater called to him.

"Really can't stay," he said cheerfully. "The ceremony begins soon, and I must be there. It was that fool Ligian's fault."

Ligian, Mr. Slater decided, would be the plump man who had stopped Elor in the morning.

"He's so careless," Elor went on. "Can you imagine a competent astrologer making a mistake of a week in the conjugation of Saturn with Scorpio? No matter. We hold the ceremony tonight, short-handed or not."

"Could I come?" Mr. Slater asked, without hesitation. "I mean, if you're short-handed—"

"Well," Elor mused. "It's unprecedented."

"I'd really like to," Mr. Slater said, seeing a chance to get to the bottom of the mystery.

"I really don't think it's fair to you," Elor went on, his thin, dark face thoughtful. "Without preparation and all—"

"I'll be all right," Mr. Slater insisted. He would really have something to dump in the mayor's lap if this worked! "I really want to go. You've got me quite excited about it."

"All right," Elor said. "We'd better hurry."

They walked down Oak Street, toward the center of town. Then, just as they reached the first stores, Elor turned. He led Mr. Slater two blocks over and a block down, and then retraced a block. After that he headed back toward the railroad station.

It was getting quite dark.

"Isn't there a simpler way?" Mr. Slater asked.

"Oh, no," Elor said. "This is the most direct. If you knew the roundabout way I came the first time—"

They walked on, backtracking blocks, circling, recrossing streets they had already passed, going back and forth over the town Mr. Slater knew so well.

But as it grew darker, and as they approached familiar streets from unfamiliar directions, Mr. Slater became just a trifle confused. He knew where he was, of course, but the constant circling had thrown him off.

How very strange, he thought. One can get lost in one's own town, even after living there almost twenty years.

Mr. Slater tried to place what street they were on without looking at the sign post, and then they made another unexpected turn. He had just made up his mind that they were backtracking on Walnut Lane, when he found that he couldn't remember the next cross street. As they passed the corner, he looked at the sign.

It read: Left Orifice.

Mr. Slater couldn't remember any street in North Ambrose called Left Orifice.

There were no streetlights on it, and Mr. Slater found

that he didn't recognize any of the stores. That was strange, because he thought he knew the little business section of North Ambrose very well. It gave him quite a start when they passed one squat black building on which there was a dimly lighted sign.

The sign read: *Temple of the Dark Mysteries of Isis.*

"They're pretty quiet in there tonight, eh?" Elor said, following Mr. Slater's glance toward the building. "We'd better hurry." He walked faster, allowing Mr. Slater no time to ask questions.

The buildings became stranger and stranger as they walked down the dim street. They were of all shapes and sizes, some new and glistening, others ancient and decayed. Mr. Slater couldn't imagine any section in North Ambrose like this. Was there a town within the town? Could there be a North Ambrose by night that the daytime inhabitants knew nothing of? A North Ambrose approached only by devious turns through familiar streets?

"Phallic rites in there," Elor said, indicating a tall, slender building. Beside it was a twisted, sagging hulk of a place.

"That's Damballa's place," Elor said, pointing at it.

Toward the end of the street was a white building. It was quite long, and built low to the ground. Mr. Slater hadn't time to examine it, because Elor had his arm and was hurrying him in the door.

"I really must become more prompt," Elor muttered half to himself.

Once inside, it was totally dark. Mr. Slater could feel movement around him, and then he made out a tiny white light. Elor guided him toward it, saying in friendly tones, "You've really helped me out of a jam."

"Have you got it?" a thin voice asked from beside the light. Mr. Slater began to make out shapes. As his eyes became more accustomed to the gloom, he could see a tiny, gnarled old man in front of the light.

The old man was holding an unusually long knife.

"Of course," Elor said. "And he was willing, too."

The white light was suspended over a stone altar, Mr. Slater realized. In a single reflex action he turned to run, but Elor's hand was tight on his arm.

"You can't leave us now," Elor said gently. "We're ready to begin."

And then there were other hands on Mr. Slater, many of them, pulling him steadily toward the Altar.

SHAPE

Pid the Pilot slowed the ship almost to a standstill. He peered anxiously at the green planet below.

Even without instruments, there was no mistaking it. Third from its sun, it was the only planet in this system capable of sustaining life. Peacefully it swam through its gauze of clouds.

It looked very innocent. And yet, something on this expedition had claimed the lives of every expedition the Glom had sent.

Pid hesitated a moment, before starting irrevocably down. He and his two crewmen were as ready now as they would ever be. Their compact Displacers were stored in body pouches, inactive but ready.

Pid wanted to say something to his crew, but wasn't sure how to put it.

The crew waited. Ilg the Radioman had sent the final

message to the Glom planet. Ger the Detector read sixteen dials at once, and reported, "No sign of alien activity." His body surfaces flowed carelessly.

Pid noticed the flow, and knew what he had to say. Ever since they had left Glom, Shape-discipline had been disgustingly lax. The Invasion Chief had warned him; but still, he had to do something about it. It was his duty, since lower castes such as Radiomen and Detectors were notoriously prone to Shapelessness.

"A lot of hopes are resting on this expedition," he began slowly. "We're a long way from home now."

Ger the Detector nodded. Ilg the Radioman flowed out of his prescribed shape and molded himself comfortably to a wall.

"However," Pid said sternly, "Distance is no excuse for promiscuous shapelessness."

Ilg flowed hastily back into proper Radioman's shape.

"Exotic shapes will undoubtedly be called for," Pid went on. "And for that we have a special dispensation. But remember—any shape not assumed strictly in the line of duty is a device of The Shapeless One!"

Ger's body surfaces abruptly stopped flowing.

"That's all," Pid said, and flowed into his controls. The ship started down, so smoothly coordinated that Pid felt a glow of pride.

They were good workers, he decided. He just couldn't expect them to be as shape-conscious as a high-caste Pilot. Even the Invasion Chief had told him that.

"Pid," the Invasion Chief had said at their last interview, "We need this planet desperately."

"Yes sir," Pid had said, standing at full attention, never quivering from Optimum Pilot's Shape.

"One of you," the Chief said heavily, "must get through and set up a Displacer near an atomic power source. The army will be standing by at this end, ready to step through."

"We'll do it, Sir," Pid said.

"This expedition has to succeed," the Chief said, and his features blurred momentarily from sheer fatigue. "In strictest confidence, there's considerable unrest on Glom. The miner caste is on strike, for instance. They want a new digging shape. Say the old one is inefficient."

Pid looked properly indignant. The Mining Shape had been set down by the ancients fifty thousand years ago, together with the rest of the basic shapes. And now these upstarts wanted to change it!

"That's not all," the Chief told him. "We've uncovered a new Cult of Shapelessness. Picked up almost eight thousand Glom, and I don't know how many more we missed."

Pid knew that Shapelessness was a lure of The Shapeless One, the greatest evil that the Glom mind conceived of. But how, he wondered, did Glom fall for His lures?

The Chief guessed his question. "Pid," he said, "I suppose it's difficult for you to understand. Do you enjoy Piloting?"

"Yes sir," Pid said simply. *Enjoy* Piloting! It was his entire life! Without a ship, he was nothing.

"Not all Glom feel that way," the Chief said. "I don't understand it either. All my ancestors have been Invasion Chiefs, back to the beginning of time. So of course *I* want to be an Invasion Chief. It's only natural, as well as lawful. But the lower castes don't feel that way." He shook his body sadly.

"I've told you this for a reason," the Chief went on. "We Glom need more room. This unrest is caused purely by crowding. All our psychologists say so. Another planet to expand into will cure everything. So we're counting on you, Pid."

"Yes sir," Pid said, with a glow of pride.

The Chief rose to end the interview. Then he changed his mind and sat down again.

"You'll have to watch your crew," he said. "They're

loyal, no doubt, but low-caste. And you know the lower castes."

Pid did indeed.

"Ger, your Detector, is suspected of harboring Alterationist tendencies. He was once fined for assuming a quasi-Hunter shape. Ilg has never had any definite charge brought against him. But I hear that he remains immobile for suspiciously long periods of time. Possibly, he fancies himself a Thinker."

"But sir," Pid protested, "If they are even slightly tainted with Alterationism or Shapelessness, why send them on this expedition?"

The Chief hesitated before answering. "There are plenty of Glom I could trust," he said slowly. "But those two have certain qualities of resourcefulness and imagination that will be needed on this expedition." He sighed. "I really don't understand why those qualities are usually linked with Shapelessness."

"Yes sir," Pid said.

"Just watch them."

"Yes sir," Pid said again, and saluted, realizing that the interview was at an end. In his body pouch he felt the dormant Displacer, ready to transform the enemy's power source into a bridge across space for the Glom hordes.

"Good luck," the chief said. "I'm sure you'll need it."

The ship dropped silently toward the surface of the enemy planet. Ger the Detector analyzed the clouds below, and fed data into the Camouflage Unit. The Unit went to work. Soon the ship looked, to all outward appearances, like a cirrus formation.

Pid allowed the ship to drift slowly toward the surface of the mystery planet. He was in Optimum Pilot's Shape now, the most efficient of the four shapes alloted to the Pilot Caste. Blind deaf and dumb, an extension of his controls, all his attention was directed toward matching the velocities of the high-flying clouds, staying among them, becoming a part of them.

Ger remained rigidly in one of the two shapes alloted to Detectors. He fed data into the Camouflage Unit, and the descending ship slowly altered into an alto-cumulus.

There was no sign of activity from the enemy planet.

Ilg located an atomic power source, and fed the data to Pid. The Pilot altered course. He had reached the lowest level of clouds, barely a mile above the surface of the planet. Now his ship looked like a fat, fleecy cumulus.

And still there was no sign of alarm. The unknown fate that had overtaken twenty previous expeditions still had not showed itself.

Dusk crept across the face of the planet as Pid maneuvered near the atomic power installation. He avoided the surrounding homes and hovered over a clump of woods.

Darkness fell, and the green planet's lone moon was veiled in clouds. .

One cloud floated lower.

And landed.

"Quick, everyone out!" Pid shouted, detaching himself from the ship's controls. He assumed the Pilot's Shape best suited for running, and raced out of the hatch. Ger and Ilg hurried after him. They stopped fifty yards from the ship, and waited.

Inside the ship a circuit closed. There was a silent shudder, and the ship began to melt. Plastic dissolved, metal crumpled. Soon the ship was a great pile of junk, and still the process went on. Big fragments broke into smaller fragments, and split, and split again.

Pid felt suddenly helpless, watching his ship scuttle itself. He was a Pilot, of the Pilot Caste. His father had been a Pilot, and his father before him, stretching back to the hazy past when the Glom had first constructed ships. He had spent his entire childhood around ships, his entire manhood flying them.

Now, shipless, he was naked in an alien world.

In a few minutes there was only a mound of dust to show where the ship had been. The night wind scattered it through the forest. And then there was nothing at all.

They waited. Nothing happened. The wind sighed and the trees creaked. Squirrels chirped, and birds stirred in their nests.

An acorn fell to the ground.

Pid heaved a sigh of relief and sat down. The twenty-first Glom expedition had landed safely.

There was nothing to be done until morning, so Pid began to make plans. They had landed as close to the atomic power installation as they dared. Now they would have to get closer. Somehow, one of them had to get very near the reactor room, in order to activate the Displacer.

Difficult. But Pid felt certain of success. After all, the Glom were strong on ingenuity.

Strong on ingenuity, he thought bitterly, but terribly short of radioactives. That was another reason why this expedition was so important. There was little radioactive fuel left, on any of the Glom worlds.

Ages ago, the Glom had spent their store of radioactives spreading throughout their neighbor worlds, occupying the ones that they could live on. Colonization barely kept up with the mounting birthrate. New worlds were constantly needed.

This particular world, discovered in a scouting expedition, was needed. It suited the Glom perfectly. But it was too far away. They didn't have enough fuel to mount a conquering space fleet.

Luckily, there was another way. A better way.

Over the centuries, the Glom scientists had developed the Displacer. A triumph of Identity Engineering, the Displacer allowed mass to be moved instantaneously between any two linked points.

One end was set up at Glom's sole atomic energy plant. The other end had to be placed in proximity to another atomic power source, and activated. Diverted power then flowed through both ends, was modified, and modified again.

Then, through the miracle of Identity Engineering, the Glom could *step* through from planet to planet; or pour through in a great, overwhelming wave.

It was quite simple. But twenty expeditions had failed to set up the Earth-end Displacer.

What had happened to them was not known.

For no Glom ship had ever returned to tell.

Before dawn they crept through the woods, taking on the coloration of the plants around them. Their Displacers pulsed feebly, sensing the nearness of atomic energy.

A tiny, four-legged creature darted in front of them. Instantly, Ger grew four legs and a long, streamlined body and gave chase.

"Ger! Come back here!" Pid howled at the Detector, throwing caution to the winds.

Ger overtook the animal and knocked it down. He tried to bite it, but he had neglected to grow teeth. The animal jumped free, and vanished into the underbrush. Ger thrust out a set of teeth and bunched his muscles for a leap.

"Ger!"

Reluctantly, the Detector turned away. He loped silently back to Pid.

"I was hungry," he said.

"You were not," Pid said sternly.

"Was," Ger mumbled, writhing with embarrassment.

Pid remembered what the Chief had told him. Ger certainly did have Hunter tendencies. He would have to watch him more closely.

"We'll have no more of that," Pid said. "Remember—the lure of Exotic Shapes is not sanctioned. Be content with the shape you were born to."

Ger nodded, and melted back into the underbrush. They moved on.

At the extreme edge of the woods they could observe the atomic energy installation. Pid disguised himself as a clump of shrubbery and Ger formed himself into an old log. Ilg, after a moment's thought, became a young oak.

The installation was in the form of a long, low building, surrounded by a metal fence. There was a gate, and guards in front of it.

The first job, Pid thought, was to get past that gate. He began to consider ways and means.

From the fragmentary reports of the survey parties, Pid knew that, in some ways, this race of Men were like the Glom. They had pets, as the Glom did, and homes and children, and a culture. The inhabitants were skilled mechanically, as were the Glom.

But there were terrific differences. The Men were of fixed and immutable forms, like stones or trees. And to compensate, their planet boasted a fantastic array of species, types and kinds. This was completely unlike Glom, which had only eight distinct forms of animal life.

And evidently, the Men were skilled at detecting invaders, Pid thought. He wished he knew how the other expeditions had failed. It would make his job much easier.

A Man lurched past them on two incredibly stiff legs. Rigidity was evident in his every move. Without looking, he hurried past.

"I know," Ger said, after the creature had moved away. "I'll disguise myself as a Man, walk through the gate to the reactor room, and activate my Displacer."

"You can't speak their language," Pid pointed out.

"I won't speak at all. I'll ignore them. Look." Quickly Ger shaped himself into a Man.

"That's not bad," Pid said.

Ger tried a few practice steps, copying the bumpy walk of the Man.

"But I'm afraid it won't work," Pid said.

"It's perfectly logical," Ger pointed out.

"I know. Therefore the other expeditions must have tried it. And none of them came back."

There was no arguing that. Ger flowed back into the shape of a log. "What, then?" he asked.

"Let me think," Pid said.

Another creature lurched past, on four legs instead of two. Pid recognized it as a Dog, a pet of Man. He watched it carefully.

The Dog ambled to the gate, head down, in no particular hurry. It walked through, unchallenged, and lay down in the grass.

"Hmm," Pid said.

They watched. One of the Men walked past, and touched the Dog on the head. The Dog stuck out its tongue, and rolled over on its side.

"I can do that," Ger said excitedly. He started to flow into the shape of a Dog.

"No, wait," Pid said. "We'll spend the rest of the day thinking it over. This is too important to rush into."

Ger subsided sulkily.

"Come on, let's move back," Pid said. He and Ger started into the woods. Then he remembered Ilg.

"Ilg?" he called softly.

There was no answer.

"Ilg!"

"What? Oh, yes," an oak tree said, and melted into a bush. "Sorry. What were you saying?"

"We're moving back," Pid said. "Were you, by any chance, Thinking?"

"Oh, no," Ilg assured him. "Just resting."

Pid let it go at that. There was too much else to worry about.

They discussed it for the rest of the day, hidden in the deepest part of the woods. The only alternatives seemed to be Man or Dog. A Tree couldn't walk past the gates, since that was not in the nature of trees. Nor could anything else, and escape notice.

Going as a Man seemed too risky. They decided that Ger would sally out in the morning as a Dog.

"Now get some sleep," Pid said.

Obediently his two crewmen flattened out, going immediately Shapeless. But Pid had a more difficult time.

Everything looked too easy. Why wasn't the atomic installation better guarded? Certainly the Men must have learned something from the expeditions they had captured in the past. Or had they killed them without asking any questions?

You couldn't tell what an alien would do.

Was that open gate a trap?

Wearily he flowed into a comfortable position on the lumpy ground. Then he pulled himself together hastily.

He had gone Shapeless!

Comfort had nothing to do with duty, he reminded himself, and firmly took a Pilot's Shape.

But Pilot's Shape wasn't constructed for sleeping on damp, bumpy ground. Pid spent a restless night, thinking of ships, and wishing he were flying one.

Pid awoke in the morning tired and ill-tempered. He nudged Ger.

"Let's get this over with," he said.

Ger flowed gaily to his feet.

"Come on, Ilg," Pid said angrily, looking around. "Wake up."

There was no reply.

"Ilg!" he called.

Still there was no reply.

"Help me look for him," Pid said to Ger. "He must be around here somewhere."

Together they tested every bush, tree, log and shrub in the vicinity. But none of them was Ilg.

Pid began to feel a cold panic run through him. What could have happened to the Radioman?

"Perhaps he decided to go through the gate on his own," Ger suggested.

Pid considered the possibility. It seemed unlikely. Ilg had never shown much initiative. He had always been content to follow orders.

They waited. But mid-day came, and there was still no sign of Ilg.

"We can't wait any longer," Pid said, and they started through the woods. Pid wondered if Ilg *had* tried to get through the gates on his own. Those quiet types often concealed a foolhardy streak.

But there was nothing to show that Ilg had been successful. He would have to assume that the Radioman was dead, or captured by the Men.

That left two of them to activate a Displacer.

And still he didn't know what had happened to the other expeditions.

At the edge of the woods, Ger turned himself into a facsimile of a Dog. Pid inspected him carefully.

"A little less tail," he said.

Ger shortened his tail.

"More ears."

Ger lenghtened his ears.

"Now even them up." He inspected the finished product. As far as he could tell, Ger was perfect, from the tip of his tail to his wet, black nose.

"Good luck," Pid said.

"Thanks." Cautiously Ger moved out of the woods,

walking in the lurching style of Dogs and Men. At the gate the guard called to him. Pid held his breath.

Ger walked past the Man, ignoring him. The Man started to walk over, and Ger broke into a run.

Pid shaped a pair of strong legs for himself, ready to dash if Ger was caught.

But the guard turned back to his gate. Ger stopped running immediately, and strolled quietly toward the main gate.

Pid dissolved his legs with a sigh of relief.

But the main door was closed! Pid hoped the Radio-man wouldn't try to open it. That was *not* in the nature of Dogs.

Another Dog came running toward Ger. Ger backed away from him. The Dog approached and sniffed. Ger sniffed back.

Then both of them ran around the building.

That was clever, Pid thought. There was bound to be a door in the rear.

He glanced up at the afternoon sun. As soon as the Displacer was activated, the Glom armies would begin to pour through. By the time the Men recovered from the shock, a million or more Glom troops would be here. With more following.

The day passed slowly, and nothing happened.

Nervously Pid watched the front of the plant. It shouldn't be taking so long, if Ger were successful.

Late into the night he waited. Men walked in and out of the installation, and Dogs barked around the gates. But Ger did not appear.

Ger had failed. Ilg was gone. Only he was left.

And *still* he didn't know what had happened.

By morning, Pid was in complete despair. He knew that the twenty-first Glom expedition to this planet was near the point of complete failure. Now it was all up to him.

He decided to sally out boldly in the shape of a Man. It was the only possibility left.

He saw that workers were arriving in great numbers, rushing through the gates. Pid wondered if he should try to mingle with them, or wait until there was less commotion. He decided to take advantage of the apparent confusion, and started to shape himself into a Man.

A Dog walked past the woods where he was hiding.

"Hello," the Dog said.

It was Ger!

"What happened?" Pid asked, with a sigh of relief. "Why were you so long? Couldn't you get in?"

"I don't know," Ger said, wagging his tail. "I didn't try."

Pid was speechless.

"I went hunting," Ger said complacently. "This form is ideal for Hunting, you know. I went out the rear gate with another Dog."

"But the expedition—your duty—"

"I changed my mind," Ger told him. "You know, Pilot, I never wanted to be a Detector."

"But you were *born* a Detector!"

"That's true," Ger said. "But it doesn't help. I always wanted to be a Hunter."

Pid shook his entire body in annoyance. "You can't," he said, very slowly, as one would explain to a Glomling. "The Hunter shape is forbidden to you."

"Not here it isn't," Ger said, still wagging his tail.

"Let's have no more of this." Pid said angrily. "Get into that installation and set up your Displacer. I'll try to overlook this heresy."

"I won't," Ger said. "I don't want the Glom here. They'd ruin it for the rest of us."

"He's right," an oak tree said.

"Ilg!" Pid gasped. "Where are you?"

Branches stirred. "I'm right here," Ilg said. "I've been Thinking."

"But—your caste—"

"Pilot," Ger said sadly, "Why don't you wake up? Most of the people on Glom are miserable. Only custom makes us take the caste-shape of our ancestors."

"Pilot," Ilg said, "All Glom are born Shapeless!"

"And being born Shapeless, all Glom should have Freedom of Shape," Ger said.

"Exactly," Ilg said. "But he'll never understand. Now excuse me. I want to Think." And the oak tree was silent.

Pid laughed humorlessly. "The Men will kill you off," he said. "Just as they killed off the rest of the expeditions."

"No one from Glom has been killed," Ger told him. "The other expeditions are right here."

"Alive?"

"Certainly. The Men don't even know we exist. That Dog I was Hunting with is a Glom from the nineteenth expedition. There are hundreds of us here, Pilot. We like it."

Pid tried to absorb it all. He had always known that the lower castes were lax in caste-consciousness. But this —this was preposterous!

This planet's secret menace was—freedom!

"Join us, Pilot," Ger said. "We've got a paradise here. Do you know how many species there are on this planet? An uncountable number! There's a shape to suit every need!"

Pid shook his head. There was no shape to suit *his* need. He was a Pilot.

But Men were unaware of the presence of the Glom. Getting near the reactor would be simple!

"The Glom Supreme Council will take care of all of you," he snarled, and shaped himself into a Dog. "I'm going to set up the Displacer myself."

He studied himself for a moment, bared his teeth at Ger, and loped toward the gate.

The Men at the gate didn't even look at him. He

slipped through the main door of the building behind a man, and loped down a corridor.

The Displacer in his body pouch pulsed and tugged, leading him toward the reactor room.

He sprinted up a flight of stairs and down another corridor. There were footsteps around the bend, and Pid knew instinctively that Dogs were not allowed inside the building.

He looked around desperately for a hiding place, but the corridor was bare. However, there were several overhead lights in the ceiling.

Pid leaped, and glued himself to the ceiling. He shaped himself into a lighting fixture, and hoped that the Men wouldn't try to find out why he wasn't shining.

Men passed, running.

Pid changed himself into a facsimile of a Man, and hurried on.

He had to get closer.

Another Man came down the corridor. He looked sharply at Pid, started to speak, and then sprinted away.

Pid didn't know what was wrong, but he broke into a full sprint. The Displacer in his body pouch throbbed and pulsed, telling him he had almost reached the critical distance.

Suddenly a terrible doubt assailed his mind. *All the expeditions had deserted! Every single Glom!*

He slowed slightly.

Freedom of Shape . . . that was a strange notion. A disturbing notion.

And obviously a device of The Shapeless One, he told himself, and rushed on.

At the end of the corridor was a gigantic bolted door. Pid stared at it.

Footsteps hammered down the corridor, and Men were shouting.

What was wrong? How had they detected him? Quickly he examined himself, and ran his fingers across his face.

He had forgotten to mold any features.

In despair he pulled at the door. He took the tiny Displacer out of his pouch, but the pulse beat wasn't quite strong enough. He had to get closer to the reactor.

He studied the door. There was a tiny crack running under it. Pid went quickly shapeless and flowed under, barely squeezing the Displacer through.

Inside the room he found another bolt on the inside of the door. He jammed it into place, and looked around for something to prop against the door.

It was a tiny room. On one side was a lead door, leading toward the reactor. There was a small window on another side, and that was all.

Pid looked at the Displacer. The pulse beat was right. At last he was close enough. Here the Displacer could work, drawing and altering the energy from the reactor. All he had to do was activate it.

But they had all deserted, every one of them.

Pid hesitated. *All Glom are born Shapeless.* That was true. Glom children were amorphous, until old enough to be instructed in the caste-shape of their ancestors. But Freedom of Shape?

Pid considered the possibilities. To be able to take on any shape he wanted, without interference! On this paradise planet he could fulfill any ambition, become anything, do anything.

Nor would he be lonely. There were other Glom here as well, enjoying the benefits of Freedom of Shape.

The Men were beginning to break down the door. Pid was still uncertain.

What should he do? Freedom . . .

But not for him, he thought bitterly. It was easy enough to be a Hunter or a Thinker. But he was a Pilot. Piloting was his life and love. How could he do that here?

Of course, the Men had ships. He could turn into a Man, find a ship . . .

Never. Easy enough to become a Tree or a Dog. He could never pass successfully as a Man.

The Door was beginning to splinter from repeated blows.

Pid walked to the window to take a last look at the planet before activating the Displacer.

He looked—and almost collapsed from shock.

It was really true! He hadn't fully understood what Ger had meant when he said that there were species on this planet to satisfy every need. *Every* need! Even his!

Here he could satisfy a longing of the Pilot Caste that went even deeper than Piloting.

He looked again, then smashed the Displacer to the floor. The door burst open, and in the same instant he flung himself through the window.

The Men raced to the window and stared out. But they were unable to understand what they saw.

There was only a great white bird out there, flapping awkwardly but with increasing strength, trying to overtake a flight of birds in the distance.

THE
IMPACTED MAN

TO: CENTER
*   Office 41*
ATTN: Controller Miglese
FROM: Contractor Carienomen
SUBJ: ATTALA Metagalaxy
Dear Controller Miglese:
*   This is to inform you that I have completed contract*
13371A. In the region of space coded ATTALA I have

constructed one metagalaxy, incorporating 549 billion galaxies, with the normal distribution of star clusters, variables, novae, et cetera. See attached data sheet.

The outer limits of ATTALA metagalaxy are defined in the accompanying map.

Speaking for myself, as chief designer, and for my company, I am confident that we have done a sound construction job, as well as a work of great artistic merit.

We welcome your inspection.

Having fulfilled the terms of our contract, the agreed-upon fee is payable at any time.

Respectfully,
Carienomen

Enclosed:
1 data sheet, installations
1 map of metagalaxy ATTALA

TO: Construction Headquarters
*   334132, Extension 12*
ATTN: Chief Designer, Carienomen
FROM: Asst. Controller Miglese
SUBJ: ATTALA Metagalaxy
Dear Carienomen:

We have inspected your construction, and have held up your fee accordingly. Artistic! I suppose it's artistic. But haven't you forgotten our prime concern in construction work?

Consistency, just to remind you.

Our inspectors discovered large amounts of unexplained data occurring even around the metagalactic center, a region one would think you would build with care. That can't go on. Luckily, the region is unpopulated.

And that's not all. Would you care to explain your spatial phenomena? What in chaos is this red shift you've built in? I've read your explanation of it, and it doesn't make any sense to me. How will planetary observers take it?

Artistry is no excuse.

Furthermore, what kinds of atoms are you using? Carienomen, are you trying to save money with shoddy materials? A good percentage of those atoms were unstable! They break down at the touch of a finger, or even without the touch of a finger. Couldn't you figure out any other way of lighting your suns?

Enclosed is a data sheet, outlining the findings of our inspectors. No payment until they're cleared up.

And there is another serious matter, just brought to my attention. Evidently you weren't watching too closely for stresses and strains in your spatial fabric. We have detected a time-flaw near the periphery of one of your galaxies. It is small, at present, but it could grow. I suggest that you take care of it at once, before you have to rebuild a galaxy or two.

One of the inhabitants of a planet impinging on the flaw is impacted already; wedged into the flaw, due entirely to your carelessness. I suggest that you correct this before he moves out of his normal time-sequence, creating paradoxes right and left.

Get in touch with him, if need be.

Also, I have word of unexplained phenomena on some of your planets; items such as flying pigs, moving mountains, ghosts, and others, all enumerated in the complaint sheet.

We won't have this sort of thing, Carienomen. A paradox is strictly forbidden in the created galaxies, since a paradox is the inevitable forerunner of chaos.

Take care of that impaction at once. I don't know whether the impacted individual realizes it yet.

                                                        Miglese

Enclosed:
1 complaint sheet

Kay Masrin folded the last blouse into the suitcase, and, with her husband's assistance, closed it.

"That's that," Jack Masrin said, hefting the bulging case. "Say good-by to the old homestead." They looked around at the furnished room where they had spent their last year.

"Good-by, homestead," Kay said. "Let's not miss the train."

"Plenty of time." Masrin started to the door. "Shall we say good-by to Happy Boy?" They had given Mr. Harf, their landlord, that nickname because he smiled, once a month, when they handed him the rent. Of course, he immediately reshaped his mouth to its usual prim line.

"Let's not," Kay said, smoothing out her tailored suit. "He just might wish us luck, and what would happen then?"

"You're perfectly right," Masrin said. "No use starting a new life with Happy Boy's blessings. I'd rather have the Witch of Endor curse me."

With Kay following him, Masrin walked to the head of the stairs. He looked down at the first floor landing, started to take the first step, and stopped abruptly.

"What's wrong?" Kay asked.

"Have we forgotten anything?" Masrin asked, frowning.

"I checked all the drawers and under the bed. Come on, we'll be late."

Masrin looked down the stairs again. Something was bothering him. He searched quickly for the source of the trouble. Of course, they had practically no money. But that had never worried him in the past. He *did* have a teaching job, finally, even if it was in Iowa. That was the important thing, after a year of working in a bookstore. Everything was going right. Why should he be worried?

He took a step down, and stopped again. The feeling was stronger. There was something he shouldn't do. He glanced back at Kay.

"Do you hate leaving that much?" Kay asked. "Let's go, or Happy Boy'll charge us another month's rent. Which, for some strange reason, we haven't got."

Still Masrin hesitated. Kay pushed past him and trotted downstairs.

"See?" she said from the first floor landing. "It's easy. Come on. Walk to Mummy."

Masrin mumbled a few subdued curses and started down the stairs. The feeling became stronger.

He reached the eighth step, and—

He was standing on a grassy plain. The transition was as sudden as that.

He gasped and blinked. The suitcase was still in his hand. But where was the brownstone? Where was Kay? Where, for that matter, was New York?

In the distance was a small blue mountain. There was a clump of trees nearby. In front of the clump was a dozen or so men.

Masrin was in a dreamlike state of shock. He observed, almost idly, that the men were short, swarthy, thickly muscled. They wore loin cloths, and carried beautifully carved and polished clubs.

They were watching him, and Masrin decided it was a tossup, who was the most surprised.

Then one of them grunted something, and they started moving toward him.

A club bounced off his suitcase.

The shock dissolved. Masrin turned, dropped the suitcase and ran like a greyhound. A club whacked his spine, nearly knocking him over. He was facing a little hill, and he bounded up it, arrows showering around him.

A few feet up, he realized that he was back in New York.

He was at the top of the stairs, still in full stride, and before he could stop himself he had run into the wall.

Kay was on the first floor landing, looking up. She gasped when she saw him, but didn't say anything.

Masrin looked at the familiar murky mauve walls of the brownstone, and at his wife.

No savages.

"What happened?" Kay whispered, white-faced, coming up the stairs.

"What did you see?" Masrin asked. He didn't have a chance to feel the full impact of what had happened. Ideas were pouring into his head, theories, conclusions.

Kay hesitated, gnawing at her lower lip. "You walked down a couple of steps and then you were gone. I couldn't see you any more. I just stood there and looked and looked. And then I heard a noise, and you were back on the stairs. Running."

They walked back to their room and opened the door. Kay sat down at once on the bed. Masrin walked around, catching his breath. Ideas were still pouring in, and he was having trouble sifting them.

"You won't believe me," he said.

"Oh won't I? Try me!"

He told her about the savages.

"You could tell me you were on Mars," Kay said. "I'd believe you. I saw you disappear!"

"My suitcase!" Masrin said suddenly, remembering that he had dropped it.

"Forget the suitcase," Kay said.

"I have to go back for it," Masrin said.

"No!"

"I must. Look, dear, it's pretty obvious what happened. I walked through some sort of time-flaw, which sent me back to the past. I must have landed in prehistoric times, to judge by the welcoming committee I met. I have to go back for that suitcase."

"Why?" Kay asked.

"Because I can't allow a paradox to occur." Masrin

didn't even wonder how he knew this. His normal ego-
tism saved him from wondering how the idea had origin-
ated in his mind.

"Look," he said, "my suitcase lands in the past. In it
I've got an electric shaver, some pants with zippers, a
plastic hairbrush, a nylon shirt, and a dozen or so books
—some of them published as late as 1951. I've even got
Ettison's 'Western Ways' in there, a text on Western
civilization from 1490 to the present day.

"The contents of that case could give these savages the
impetus to change their own history. And suppose some
of that stuff got into the hands of Europeans, after they
discovered America? How would that affect the present?"

"I don't know," Kay said. "And you don't either."

"Of course I know," Masrin said. It was all crystal-
clear. He was amazed that she wasn't able to follow it
logically.

"Look at it this way," Masrin said. "Minutiae makes
history. The present is made up of a tremendous number
of infinitesmal factors, which shaped and molded the
past. If you add another factor to the past, you're bound
to get another result in the present. But the present is as
it is, unchangeable. So we have a paradox. And there
can't be any paradox!"

"Why can't there?" Kay asked.

Masrin frowned. For a bright girl, she was following
him very poorly. "Just believe me," he said. "Paradox
isn't allowed in a logical universe." Allowed by whom?
He had the answer.

"The way I see it," Masrin said, "there must be a regu-
lating principle in the universe. All our natural laws are
expressions of it. This principle can't stand paradox, because . . . because—" He knew that the answer had to do
with suppressing the fundamental chaos, but he didn't
know why.

"Anyhow, this principle can't stand paradox."

"Where did you get that idea?" Kay asked. She had never heard Jack talk that way before.

"I've had these ideas for a long time," Masrin said, and believed it. "There was just never any reason to talk about it. Anyhow, I'm going back for my suitcase."

He walked out to the landing, followed by Kay. "Sorry I can't bring you any souvenirs," Masrin said cheerfully. "Unfortunately, that would result in a paradox also. Everything in the past has had a part in shaping the present. Remove something, and it's like removing one unknown from an equation. You wouldn't get the same result." He started down the stairs.

On the eighth step, he disappeared again.

He was back in prehistoric America. The savages were gathered around the suitcase, only a few feet from him. They hadn't opened it yet, Masrin noticed thankfully. Of course, the suitcase itself was a pretty paradoxical article. But its appearance—and his—would probably be swallowed up in myth and legend. Time had a certain amount of flexibility.

Looking at them, Masrin couldn't decide if they were forerunners of Indians, or a separate sub-race which didn't survive. He wondered if they thought he was an enemy, or a garden-variety evil spirit.

Masrin darted forward, shoved two of them aside, and grabbed his suitcase. He ran back, circling the little hill, and stopped.

He was still in the past.

Where in chaos was that hole in time, Masrin wondered, not noticing the strangeness of his oath. The savages were coming after him now, starting around the little hill. Masrin almost had the answer, then lost it as an arrow sped past him. He sprinted, trying to keep the hill between himself and the Indians. His long legs pumped, and a club bounced behind him.

Where was that hole in time? What if it had moved? Perspiration poured from his face as he ran. A club grazed his arm, and he twisted around the side of the hill, looking wildly for shelter.

He met three squat savages, coming after him.

Masrin fell to the ground as they swung their clubs, and they tripped over his body. Others were coming now, and he jumped to his feet.

Up! The thought struck him suddenly, cutting through his fear. Up!

He charged the hill, certain that he would never reach the top alive.

And he was back in the boarding house, still holding the suitcase.

"Are you hurt, darling?" Kay put her arms around him. "What happened?"

Masrin had only one rational thought. He couldn't remember any prehistoric tribe that carved their clubs as elaborately as these savages. It was almost a unique art form, and he wished he could get one of the clubs to a museum.

Then he looked at the mauve walls wildly, expecting to see the savages come bounding out of them. Or perhaps there were little men in his suitcase. He fought for control. The thinking portion of his mind told him not to be alarmed; flaws in time were possible, and he had become wedged, impacted in one. Everything else followed logically. All he had to do—

But another part of his mind wasn't interested in logic. It had been staring blankly at the impossibility of the whole thing, uninfluenced by any rational arguments. That part knew an impossibility when it saw one, and said so.

Masrin screamed and fainted.

TO: CENTER
  Office 41
ATTN: Asst. Controller Miglese
FROM: Contractor Carienomen
SUBJ: ATTALA Metagalaxy
Dear Sir:

I consider your attitude unfair. True, I have utilized some new ideas in my approach to this particular metagalaxy. I have allowed myself the latitude of artistry, never thinking I would be beset by the howls of a static, reactionary CENTER.

Believe me, I am as interested as you in our great job— that of suppressing the fundamental chaos. But in doing this, we must not sacrifice our values.

Enclosed is a statement of defense concerning my use of the red shift, and another statement of the advantages gained by using a small percentage of unstable atoms for lighting and energy purposes.

As to the time-flaw, that was merely a small error in duration-flow, and has nothing to do with the fabric of space, which is, I assure you, of first-rate quality.

There is, as you pointed out, an individual impacted in the flaw, which makes the job of repair slightly more difficult. I have been in contact with him, indirectly of course, and have succeeded in giving him a limited understanding of his rôle.

If he doesn't disturb the flaw too much by time-traveling, I should be able to sew it up with little difficulty. I don't know if this procedure is possible, though. My rapport with him is quite shaky, and he seems to have a number of strong influences around him, counseling him to move.

I could perform an extraction of course, and ultimately I may have to do just that. For that matter, if the thing gets out of hand I may be forced to extract the entire planet. I hope not, since that would necessitate clearing that entire portion of space, where there are also local

*observers. This, in turn, might necessitate rebuilding an
entire galaxy.*

*However, I hope to have the problem settled by the
time I next communicate with you.*

*The warp in the metagalactic center was caused by
some workmen leaving a disposal unit open. It has been
closed.*

*The phenomena such as walking mountains, et cetera,
are being handled in the usual way.*

Payment is still due on my work.

Respectfully,

Carienomen

Enclosed:
1 statement, 5541 pages, Red Shift
1 statement, 7689 pages, Unstable Atoms

TO: Construction Headquarters
 334132, Extension 12
ATTN: Contractor Carienomen
FROM: Asst. Controller Miglese
SUBJ: ATTALA Metagalaxy
Carienomen:
 *You will be paid after you can show me a logical, de-
cently constructed job. I'll read your statements when and
if I have time. Take care of the flaw-impaction before it
tears a hole in the fabric of space.*

Miglese

Masrin recovered his nerve in half an hour. Kay put a
compress on a purple bruise on his arm. Masrin started
pacing the room. Once again, he was in complete posses-
sion of his faculties. Ideas started to come.

"The past is down," he said, half to Kay, half to himself.

"I don't mean really 'down'; but when I move in that
apparent direction, I step through the hole in time. It's
a case of shifted conjoined dimensionality."

"What does that mean?" Kay asked, staring wide-eyed at her husband.

"Just take my word for it," Masrin said, "I can't go down." He couldn't explain it to her any better. There weren't words to fit the concepts.

"Can you go up?" Kay asked, completely confused.

"I don't know. I suppose, if I went up, I'd go into the future."

"Oh, I can't stand it," Kay said. "What's wrong with you? How will you get out of here? How will you get down that haunted staircase?"

"Are you people still there?" Mr. Harf's voice croaked from outside. Masrin walked over and opened the door.

"I think we're going to stay for a while," he said to the landlord.

"You're not," Harf said. "I've already rented this room again." Happy Boy Harf was small and bony, with a narrow skull and lips as thin as a spider's thread. He stalked into the room, looking around for signs of damage to his property. One of Mr. Harf's little idiosyncrasies was his belief that the nicest people were capable of the worst crimes.

"When are the people coming?" Masrin asked.

"This afternoon. And I want you out before they get here."

"Couldn't we make some arrangement?" Masrin asked. The impossibility of the situation struck him. He couldn't go downstairs. If Harf forced him out, he would have to go to prehistoric New York, where he was sure his return was eagerly awaited.

And there was the over-all problem of paradox!

"I'm sick," Kay said in a stifled little voice. "I can't leave yet."

"What are you sick from? I'll call an ambulance if you're sick," Harf said, looking suspiciously around the room for any signs of bubonic plague.

"I'd gladly pay you double the rent if you'd let us stay a little longer," Masrin said.

Harf scratched his head, and stared at Masrin. He wiped his nose on the back of his hand, and said, "Where's the money?"

Masrin realized that he had about ten dollars left, and his train tickets. He and Kay were going to ask for an advance as soon as they reached the college.

"Broke," Harf said. "I thought you had a job at some school?"

"He does," Kay said staunchly.

"Then why don't you go there and get out of my place?" Harf asked.

The Masrins were silent. Harf glared at them.

"Very suspicious. Get out before noon, or I'll call a cop."

"Hold it," Masrin said. "We've paid the rent for today. The room's ours until twelve midnight."

Harf stared at them. He wiped his nose again, thoughtfully.

"Don't try staying one minute over," he said, stamping out of the room.

As soon as Harf was gone, Kay hurried over and closed the door. "Honey," she said, "why don't you call up some scientists here in New York and tell them what's happened? I'm sure they'd arrange something, until . . . how long will we have to stay here?"

"Until the flaw's repaired," Masrin said. "But we can't tell anyone; especially, we can't tell any scientists."

"Why not?" Kay asked.

"Look, the important thing, as I told you, is to avoid a paradox. That means I have to keep my hands off the past, and the future. Right?"

"If you say so," Kay said.

"We call in a team of scientists, and what happens? Naturally, they're skeptical. They want to *see* me do it. So I do it. Immediately, they bring in a few of their colleagues. *They* watch me disappear. Understand, all this time there's no proof that I've gone into the past. All they know is, if I walk downstairs, I disappear.

"Photographers are called in, to make sure I'm not hypnotizing the scientists. Then they demand proof. They want me to bring back a scalp, or one of those carved clubs. The newspapers get hold of it. It's inevitable that somewhere along the line I produce a paradox. And do you know what happens then?"

"No, and you don't either."

"I do," Masrin said firmly. "Once a paradox is caused, the agent—the man who caused it—me—disappears. For good. And it goes down in the books as another unsolved mystery. That way, the paradox is resolved in its easiest way—by getting rid of the paradoxical element."

"If you think you're in danger, then of course we won't call in any scientists," Kay said. "Although I wish I knew what you were driving at. I don't understand anything you've said." She went to the window and looked out. There was New York, and beyond it, somewhere, was Iowa, where they should be going. She looked at her watch. They had already missed the train.

"Phone the college," Masrin said. "Tell them I'll be delayed a few days."

"Will it be a few days?" Kay asked. "How will you ever get out?"

"Oh, the hole in time isn't permanent," Masrin said confidently. "It'll heal—if I don't go sticking myself in it."

"But we can only stay here until midnight. What happens then?"

"I don't know," Masrin said. "We can only hope it'll be fixed by then."

TO: CENTER
   Office 41
ATTN: Asst. Controller Miglese
FROM: Contractor Carienomen
SUBJ: MORSTT Metagalaxy
Dear Sir:
   Herein, enclosed, is my bid for work on the new meta-galaxy in the region coded MORSTT. If you have heard any discussions in art circles recently, I think that you will see that my use of unstable atoms in ATTALA Meta-galaxy has been proclaimed "the first great advance in creative engineering since the invention of variable time-flow." See the enclosed reviews.

   My artistry has stirred many favorable comments.

   Most of the inconsistencies—natural inconsistencies, let me remind you—in ATTALA Metagalaxy have been cor-rected. I am still working with the man impacted in the time flaw. He is proving quite co-operative; at least, as co-operative as he can be, with the various influences around him.

   To date, I have coalesced the edges of the flaw, and am allowing them to harden. I hope the individual remains immobile, since I really don't like to extract anyone or anything. After all, each person, each planet, each star system, no matter how minute, has an integral part in my metagalactic scheme.

   Artistically, at any rate.

   Your inspection is welcomed again. Please note the galactic configurations around the metagalactic center. They are a dream of beauty you will wish to carry with you always.

   Please consider my bid for the MORSTT Metagalaxy project in light of my past achievements.

   Payment is still due on ATTALA Metagalaxy.
                                          Respectfully,
                                              Carienomen

Enclosed:
1 bid, for MORSTT Metagalaxy project
3 critical reviews, ATTALA Metagalaxy

"It's eleven forty-five, honey," Kay said nervously. "Do you think we could go now?"

"Let's wait a few minutes longer," Masrin said. He could hear Harf prowling around on the landing, waiting eagerly for the dot of twelve.

Masrin watched the seconds tick by on his watch.

At five minutes to twelve, he decided that he might as well find out. If the hole wasn't fixed by now, another five minutes wouldn't do it.

He placed the suitcase on the dresser, and moved a chair next to it.

"What are you doing?" Kay asked.

"I don't feel like trying those stairs at night," Masrin said. "It's bad enough playing with those pre-Indians in the daylight. I'm going to try going up, instead." His wife gave him an under-the-eyelids now-I-know-you're-cracking look.

"It's not the stairs that does it," Masrin told her again. "It's the act of going up or down. The critical distance seems to be about five feet. This will do just as well."

Kay stood nervously, clenching and unclenching both hands, as Masrin climbed on the chair and put one foot on the dresser. Then the other, and he stood up.

"I think it's all right," he said, teetering a little. "I'm going to try it a little higher."

He climbed on the suitcase.

And disappeared.

It was day, and he was in a city. But the city didn't look like New York. It was breathtakingly beautiful—so beautiful that Masrin didn't dare breathe, for fear of disturbing its fragile loveliness.

It was a place of delicate, wispy towers and buildings.

And people. But what people, Masrin thought, letting out his breath with a sigh.

The people were blue-skinned. The light was green, coming from a green-tinged sun.

Masrin drew in a breath of air, and strangled. He gasped again, and started to lose his balance. There was no air in the place! At least, no air he could breathe. He felt for a step behind him, and then tumbled down—

To land, choking and writhing, on the floor of his room.

After a few moments he could breathe again. He heard Harf pounding on the door. Masrin staggered to his feet, and tried to think of something. He knew Harf; the man was probably certain by now that Masrin headed the Mafia. He would call a cop if they didn't leave. And that would ultimately result in—

"Listen," he said to Kay, "I've got another idea." His throat was burning from the atmosphere of the future. However, he told himself, there was no reason why he should be surprised. He had made quite a jump forward. The composition of the Earth's atmosphere must have changed, gradually, and the people had adapted to it. But it was a poison for him.

"There are two possibilities now," he said to Kay. "One, that under the prehistoric layer is another, earlier layer. Two, that the prehistoric layer is only a temporary discontinuity. That under it, is present New York again. Follow me?"

"No."

"I'm going to try going under the prehistoric layer. It might get me down to the ground floor. Certainly, it can't be any worse." Kay considered the logic of going some thousands of years into the past in order to walk ten feet, but didn't say anything.

Masrin opened the door and went out to the stairs, followed by Kay. "Wish me luck," he said.

"Luck, nothing," Mr. Harf said, on the landing. "Just get out of here."

Masrin plunged down the stairs.

It was still morning in prehistoric New York, and the savages were still waiting for him. Masrin estimated that only about half an hour had gone by here. He didn't have time to wonder why.

He had caught them by surprise, and was twenty yards away before they saw him. They followed, and Masrin looked for a depression. He had to go down five feet, in order to get out.

He found a shelving of the land, and jumped down.

He was in water. Not just on the surface, but *under*. The pressure was tremendous, and Masrin could not see sunlight above him.

He must have gone through to a time when this section was under the Atlantic.

Masrin kicked furiously, eardrums bursting. He started to rise toward the surface, and—

He was back on the plain, dripping wet.

This time, the savages had had enough. They looked at him, materialized in front of them, gave a shriek of horror, and bolted.

This water sprite was too strong for them.

Wearily, Masrin walked back to the hill, climbed it, and was back in the brownstone.

Kay was staring at him, and Harf's jaw was hanging slack. Masrin grinned weakly.

"Mr. Harf," he said, "will you come into my room? There's something I want to tell you."

TO: CENTER
     Office 41
ATTN: Asst. Controller Miglese
FROM: Contractor Carienomen
SUBJ: MORSTT Metagalaxy

My Dear Sir:

I cannot understand your reply to my bid for the job of constructing MORSTT Metagalaxy. Moreover, I do not think that obscenity has any place in a business letter.

If you have taken the trouble to inspect my latest work in ATTALA, you will see that it is, take it all for all, a beautiful job, and one that will go a long way toward holding back the fundamental chaos.

The only detail left to attend to is the matter of the impacted man. I fear I shall have to extract.

The flaw was hardening nicely, when he blundered into it again, tearing it worse than ever. No paradox as yet, but I can see one coming.

Unless he can control his immediate environment, and do it at once, I shall take the necessary step. Paradox is not allowed.

I consider it my duty to ask you to reconsider my bid for the MORSTT Metagalaxy project.

And I trust you will excuse me for bringing this oversight to your attention, but payment is still due.

Respectfully,

Carienomen

"So that's the story, Mr. Harf," Masrin said, an hour later. "I know how weird it sounds; but you saw me disappear yourself."

"That I did," Harf said. Masrin went into the bathroom to hang up his wet clothes.

"Yes, Harf said, "I guess you disappeared at that."

"I certainly did."

"And you don't want the scientists to know about your deal with the devil?" Harf asked slyly.

"No! I explained about paradox, and—"

"Let me see," Harf said. He wiped his nose vigorously. "Those carved clubs you said they had. Wouldn't one of those be valuable to a museum? You said there was nothing like it."

"What?" Masrin asked, coming out of the bathroom. "Listen, I can't touch any of that stuff. It'll result in—"

"Of course," Harf said, "I could call in some newspaper boys instead. And some scientists. I could probably make me a nice little pile out of this devil-worship."

"You wouldn't!" Kay said, remembering only that her husband had said something bad would happen.

"Be reasonable," Harf said. "All I want is one or two of those clubs. That won't cause any trouble. You can just ask your devil—"

"There's no devil involved," Masrin said. "You have no idea what part one of those clubs might have played in history. The club I take might have killed the man who would have united these people, and the North American Indians might have met the Europeans as a single nation. Think how that would change—"

"Don't hand me that stuff," Harf said. "Are you getting me a club or aren't you?"

"I've explained it to you," Masrin said wearily.

"And don't tell me any more about this paradox business. I don't understand it, anyhow. But I'll split fifty-fifty with you on what I get for the club."

"No."

"O.K. I'll be seeing you." Harf started for the door.

"Wait."

"Yes?" Harf's thin, spidery mouth was smiling now.

Masrin examined his choice of evils. If he brought back a club there was a good chance of starting a paradox, by removing all that the club had done in the past. But if he didn't, Harf would call in the newspapers and scientists. They could find out if Harf was speaking the truth by simply carrying him downstairs; something the police would do anyhow. He would disappear, and then—"

With more people in on it, a paradox would be inevitable. And all Earth might, very possibly, be removed. Although he didn't know why, Masrin knew this for a certainty.

He was lost either way, but getting the club seemed the simpler alternative.

"I'll get it," Masrin said. He walked to the staircase, followed by Kay and Harf. Kay grabbed his hand.

"Don't do it," she said.

"There's nothing else I can do." He thought for a moment of killing Harf. But that would only result in the electric chair for him. Of course, he could kill Harf and take his body into the past, and bury it.

But the corpse of a twentieth century man in prehistoric America might constitute a paradox anyhow. Suppose it was dug up?

Besides, he didn't have it in him to kill a man.

Masrin kissed his wife, and walked downstairs.

There were no savages in sight on the plain, although Masrin thought he could feel their eyes, watching him. He found two clubs on the ground. The ones that struck him must be taboo, he decided, and picked one up, expecting another to crush his skull any moment. But the plain was silent.

"Good boy!" Harf said. "Hand it here!" Masrin handed him the club. He went over to Kay and put his arm around her. It was a paradox now, as certainly as if he had killed his great-great-grandfather before he was born. "That's a lovely thing," Harf said, admiring the club under the light. "Consider your rent paid for the rest of the month—"

The club disappeared from his hand.

Harf disappeared.

Kay fainted.

Masrin carried her to the bed, and splashed water on her face.

"What happened?" she asked.

"I don't know," Masrin said, suddenly very puzzled about everything. "All I know is, we're going to stay here for at least two weeks. Even if we have to eat beans."

TO: CENTER
   Office 41
ATTN: Asst Controller Miglese
FROM: Contractor Càrienomen
SUBJ: MORSTT Metagalaxy
Sir:

Your offer of a job repairing damaged stars is an insult to my company and myself. We refuse. Let me point out my work in the past, outlined in the brochure I am enclosing. How can you offer so menial a job to one of CENTER'S greatest companies?

Again, I would like to put in my request for work on the new MORSTT Metagalaxy.

As for ATTALA Metagalaxy—the work is now completed, and a finer job cannot be found anywhere this side of chaos. The place is a wonder.

The impacted man is no longer impacted. I was forced to extract. However, I did not extract the man himself. Instead, I was able to remove one of the external influences on him. Now he can grow out normally.

A nice job, I think you'll admit, and solved with the ingenuity that characterizes all my work.

My decision was: Why extract a good man, when I could save him by pulling the rotten one beside him?

Again, I welcome your inspection. I request reconsideration on MORSTT Metagalaxy.

PAYMENT IS STILL DUE!

                              Respectfully,

                                        Carienomen

Enclosed:
1 brochure, 9978 pages

UNTOUCHED
BY HUMAN HANDS

HELLMAN PLUCKED THE LAST RADISH out of the can with a pair of dividers. He held it up for Casker to admire, then laid it carefully on the workbench beside the razor.

"Hell of a meal for two grown men," Casker said, flopping down in one of the ship's padded crash chairs.

"If you'd like to give up your share—" Hellman started to suggest.

Casker shook his head quickly. Hellman smiled, picked up the razor and examined its edge critically.

"Don't make a production out of it," Casker said, glancing at the ship's instruments. They were approaching a red dwarf, the only planet-bearing sun in the vicinity. "We want to be through with supper before we get much closer."

Hellman made a practice incision in the radish, squinting along the top of the razor. Casker bent closer, his mouth open. Hellman poised the razor delicately and cut the radish cleanly in half.

"Will you say grace?" Hellman asked.

Casker growled something and popped a half in his mouth. Hellman chewed more slowly. The sharp taste seemed to explode along his disused tastebuds.

"Not much bulk value," Hellman said.

Casker didn't answer. He was busily studying the red dwarf.

As he swallowed the last of his radish, Hellman stifled a sigh. Their last meal had been three days ago . . . if two biscuits and a cup of water could be called a meal. This radish, now resting in the vast emptiness of their stomachs, was the last gram of food on board ship.

"Two planets," Casker said. "One's burned to a crisp."

"Then we'll land on the other."

Casker nodded and punched a deceleration spiral into the ship's tape.

Hellman found himself wondering for the hundredth time where the fault had been. Could he have made out the food requisitions wrong, when they took on supplies at Calao station? After all, he had been devoting most of his attention to the mining equipment. Or had the ground crew just forgotten to load those last precious cases?

He drew his belt in to the fourth new notch he had punched.

Speculation was useless. Whatever the reason, they were in a jam. Ironically enough, they had more than enough fuel to take them back to Calao. But they would be a pair of singularly emaciated corpses by the time the ship reached there.

"We're coming in now," Casker said.

And to make matters worse, this unexplored region of space had few suns and fewer planets. Perhaps there was a slight possibility of replenishing their water supply, but the odds were enormous against finding anything they could eat.

"Look at that place," Casker growled.

Hellman shook himself out of his reverie.

The planet was like a round gray-brown porcupine. The spines of a million needle-sharp mountains glittered in the red dwarf's feeble light. And as they spiraled lower, circling the planet, the pointed mountains seemed to stretch out to meet them.

"It can't be *all* mountains," Hellman said.

"It's not."

Sure enough, there were oceans and lakes, out of which

thrust jagged island-mountains. But no sign of level land, no hint of civilization, or even animal life.

"At least it's got an oxygen atmosphere," Casker said.

Their deceleration spiral swept them around the planet, cutting lower into the atmosphere, braking against it. And still there was nothing but mountains and lakes and oceans and more mountains.

On the eighth run, Hellman caught sight of a solitary building on a mountain top. Casker braked recklessly, and the hull glowed red hot. On the eleventh run, they made a landing approach.

"Stupid place to build," Casker muttered.

The building was doughnut-shaped, and fitted nicely over the top of the mountain. There was a wide, level lip around it, which Casker scorched as he landed the ship.

From the air, the building had merely seemed big. On the ground, it was enormous. Hellman and Casker walked up to it slowly. Hellman had his burner ready, but there was no sign of life.

"This planet must be abandoned," Hellman said almost in a whisper.

"Anyone in his right mind would abandon this place," Casker said. "There're enough good planets around, without anyone trying to live on a needle point."

They reached the door. Hellman tried to open it and found it locked. He looked back at the spectacular display of mountains.

"You know," he said, "when this planet was still in a molten state, it must have been affected by several gigantic moons that are now broken up. The strains, external and internal, wrenched it into its present spined appearance and—"

"Come off it," Casker said ungraciously. "You were a librarian before you decided to get rich on uranium."

Hellman shrugged his shoulders and burned a hole in the doorlock. They waited.

The only sound on the mountain top was the growling of their stomachs.

They entered.

The tremendous wedge-shaped room was evidently a warehouse of sorts. Goods were piled to the ceiling, scattered over the floor, stacked haphazardly against the walls. There were boxes and containers of all sizes and shapes, some big enough to hold an elephant, others the size of thimbles.

Near the door was a dusty pile of books. Immediately, Hellman bent down to examine them.

"Must be food somewhere in here," Casker said, his face lighting up for the first time in a week. He started to open the nearest box.

"This is interesting," Hellman said, discarding all the books except one.

"Let's eat first," Casker said, ripping the top off the box. Inside was a brownish dust. Casker looked at it, sniffed, and made a face.

"Very interesting indeed," Hellman said, leafing through the book.

Casker opened a small can, which contained a glittering green slime. He closed it and opened another. It contained a dull orange slime.

"Hmm," Hellman said, still reading.

"Hellman! Will you kindly drop that book and help me find some food?"

"Food?" Hellman repeated, looking up. "What makes you think there's anything to eat here? For all you know, this could be a paint factory."

"It's a warehouse!" Casker shouted.

He opened a kidney-shaped can and lifted out a soft purple stick. It hardened quickly and crumpled to dust as he tried to smell it. He scooped up a handful of the dust and brought it to his mouth.

"That might be extract of strychnine," Hellman said casually.

Casker abruptly dropped the dust and wiped his hands.

"After all," Hellman pointed out, "granted that this is a warehouse—a cache, if you wish—we don't know what the late inhabitants considered good fare. Paris Green salad, perhaps, with sulphuric acid as dressing."

"All right," Casker said, "but we gotta eat. What're you going to do about all this?" He gestured at the hundreds of boxes, cans and bottles.

"The thing to do," Hellman said briskly, "is to make a qualitative analysis on four or five samples. We could start out with a simple titration, sublimate the chief ingredient, see if it forms a precipitate, work out its molecular makeup from—"

"Hellman, you don't know what you're talking about. You're a librarian, remember? And I'm a correspondence school pilot. We don't know anything about titrations and sublimations."

"I know," Hellman said, "but we should. It's the right way to go about it."

"Sure. In the meantime, though, just until a chemist drops in, what'll we do?"

"This might help us," Hellman said, holding up the book. "Do you know what it is?"

"No," Casker said, keeping a tight grip on his patience.

"It's a pocket dictionary and guide to the Helg language."

"Helg?"

"The planet we're on. The symbols match up with those on the boxes."

Casker raised an eyebrow. "Never heard of Helg."

"I don't believe the planet has ever had any contact with Earth," Hellman said. "This dictionary isn't Helg-English. It's Helg-Aloombrigian."

Casker remembered that Aloombrigia was the home planet of a small, adventurous reptilian race, out near the center of the Galaxy.

"How come you can read Aloombrigian?" Casker asked.

"Oh, being a librarian isn't a completely useless profession," Hellman said modestly. "In my spare time—"

"Yeah. Now how about—"

"Do you know," Hellman said, "the Aloombrigians probably helped the Helgans leave their planet and find another. They sell services like that. In which case, this building very likely *is* a food cache!"

"Suppose you start translating," Casker suggested wearily, "and maybe find us something to eat."

They opened boxes until they found a likely-looking substance. Laboriously, Hellman translated the symbols on it.

"Got it," he said. "It reads:—'Use Sniffners—The Better Abrasive.' "

"Doesn't sound edible," Casker said.

"I'm afraid not."

They found another, which read: vigroom! fill all your stomachs, and fill them right!

"What kind of animals do you suppose these Helgans were?" Casker asked.

Hellman shrugged his shoulders.

The next label took almost fifteen minutes to translate. It read: argosel makes your thudra all tizzy. contains thirty arps of ramstat pulz, for shell lubrication.

"There must be *something* here we can eat," Casker said with a note of desperation.

"I hope so," Hellman replied.

At the end of two hours, they were no closer. They had translated dozens of titles and sniffed so many substances that their olfactory senses had given up in disgust.

"Let's talk this over," Hellman said, sitting on a box marked: vormitash—good as it sounds!

"Sure," Casker said, sprawling out on the floor. "Talk."

"If we could deduce what kind of creatures inhabited this planet, we'd know what kind of food they ate, and whether it's likely to be edible for us."

"All we do know is that they wrote a lot of lousy advertising copy."

Hellman ignored that. "What kind of intelligent beings would evolve on a planet that is all mountains?"

"Stupid ones!" Casker said.

That was no help. But Hellman found that he couldn't draw any inferences from the mountains. It didn't tell him if the late Helgans ate silicates or proteins or iodine-base foods or anything.

"Now look," Hellman said, "we'll have to work this out by pure logic—Are you listening to me?"

"Sure," Casker said.

"Okay. There's an old proverb that covers our situation perfectly: 'One man's meat is another man's poison.'"

"Yeah," Casker said. He was positive his stomach had shrunk to approximately the size of a marble.

"We can assume, first, that their meat is our meat."

Casker wrenched himself away from a vision of five juicy roast beefs dancing tantalizingly before him. "What if their meat is our *poison?* What then?"

"Then," Hellman said, "we will assume that their poison is our meat."

"And what happens if their meat *and* their poison are our poison?"

"We starve."

"All right," Casker said, standing up. "Which assumption do we start with?"

"Well, there's no sense in asking for trouble. This *is* an oxygen planet, if that means anything. Let's assume that we can eat some basic food of theirs. If we can't we'll start on their poisons."

"If we live that long," Casker said.

Hellman began to translate labels. They discarded such brands as ANDROGYNITES DELIGHT and VERBELL—FOR LONGER, CURLIER, MORE SENSITIVE ANTENNAE, until they found a small gray box, about six inches by three by three. It was

called VALKORIN'S UNIVERSAL TASTE TREAT, FOR ALL DIGES-
TIVE CAPACITIES.

"This looks as good as any," Hel' an said. He opened
the box.

Casker leaned over and sniffed. "No odor."

Within the box they found a rectangular, rubbery red
block. It quivered slightly, like jelly.

"Bite into it," Casker said.

"Me?" Hellman asked. "Why not you?"

"You picked it."

"I prefer just looking at it," Hellman said with dignity.
"I'm not too hungry."

"I'm not either," Casker said.

They sat on the floor and stared at the jellylike block.
After ten minutes, Hellman yawned, leaned back and
closed his eyes.

"All right, coward," Casker said bitterly. "I'll try it.
Just remember, though, if I'm poisoned, you'll never get
off this planet. You don't know how to pilot."

"Just take a little bite, then," Hellman advised.

Casker leaned over and stared at the block. Then he
prodded it with his thumb.

The rubbery red block giggled.

"Did you hear that?" Casker yelped, leaping back.

"I didn't hear anything," Hellman said, his hands shak-
ing. "Go ahead."

Casker prodded the block again. It giggled louder, this
time with a disgusting little simper.

"Okay," Casker said, "what do we try next?"

"Next? What's wrong with this?"

"I don't eat anything that giggles," Casker stated firmly.

"Now listen to me," Hellman said. "The creatures who
manufactured this might have been trying to create an
esthetic sound as well as a pleasant shape and color. That
giggle is probably only for the amusement of the eater."

"Then bite into it yourself," Casker offered.

Hellman glared at him, but made no move toward the

rubbery block. Finally he said, "Let's move it out of the way."

They pushed the block over to a corner. It lay there giggling softly to itself.

"Now what?" Casker said.

Hellman looked around at the jumbled stacks of incomprehensible alien goods. He noticed a door on either side of the room.

"Let's have a look in the other sections," he suggested.

Casker shrugged his shoulders apathetically.

Slowly they trudged to the door in the left wall. It was locked and Hellman burned it open with the ship's burner.

It was a wedge-shaped room, piled with incomprehensible alien goods.

The hike back across the room seemed like miles, but they made it only slightly out of wind. Hellman blew out the lock and they looked in.

It was a wedge-shaped room, piled with incomprehensible alien goods.

"All the same," Casker said sadly, and closed the door.

"Evidently there's a series of these rooms going completely around the building," Hellman said. "I wonder if we should explore them."

Casker calculated the distance around the building, compared it with his remaining strength, and sat down heavily on a long gray object.

"Why bother?" he asked.

Hellman tried to collect his thoughts. Certainly he should be able to find a key of some sort, a clue that would tell him what they could eat. But where was it?

He examined the object Casker was sitting on. It was about the size and shape of a large coffin, with a shallow depression on top. It was made of a hard, corrugated substance.

"What do you suppose this is?" Hellman asked.

"Does it matter?"

Hellman glanced at the symbol painted on the side of the object, then looked them up in his dictionary.

"Fascinating," he murmured, after a while.

"Is it something to eat?" Casker asked, with a faint glimmering of hope.

"No. You are sitting on something called THE MOROG CUSTOM SUPER TRANSPORT FOR THE DISCRIMINATING HELGAN WHO DESIRES THE BEST IN VERTICAL TRANSPORTATION. It's a vehicle!"

"Oh," Casker said dully.

"This is important! Look at it! How does it work?"

Casker wearily climbed off the Morog Custom Super Transport and looked it over carefully. He traced four almost invisible separations on its four corners. "Retractable wheels, probably, but I don't see—"

Hellman read on. "It says to give it three amphus of high-gain Integor fuel, then a van of Tonder lubrication, and not to run it over three thousand Ruls for the first fifty mungus."

"Let's find something to eat," Casker said.

"Don't you see how important this is?" Hellman asked. "This could solve our problem. If we could deduce the alien logic inherent in constructing this vehicle, we might know the Helgan thought pattern. This, in turn, would give us an insight into their nervous systems, which would imply their biochemical makeup."

Casker stood still, trying to decide whether he had enough strength left to strangle Hellman.

"For example," Hellman said, "what kind of vehicle would be used in a place like this? Not one with wheels, since everything is up and down. Anti-gravity? Perhaps, but what *kind* of anti-gravity? And why did the inhabitants devise a boxlike form instead—"

Casker decided sadly that he didn't have enough strength to strangle Hellman, no matter how pleasant it might be. Very quietly, he said, "Kindly stop making like a scientist. Let's see if there isn't *something* we can gulp down."

"All right," Hellman said sulkily.

Casker watched his partner wander off among the cans, bottles and cases. He wondered vaguely where Hellman got the energy, and decided that he was just too cerebral to know when he was starving.

"Here's something," Hellman called out, standing in front of a large yellow vat.

"What does it say?" Casker asked.

"Little bit hard to translate. But rendered freely, it reads: MORISHILLE'S VOOZY, WITH LACTO-ECTO ADDED FOR A NEW TASTE SENSATION. EVERYONE DRINKS VOOZY. GOOD BEFORE AND AFTER MEALS, NO UNPLEASANT AFTER-EFFECTS. GOOD FOR CHILDREN! THE DRINK OF THE UNIVERSE!"

"That sounds good," Casker admitted, thinking that Hellman might not be so stupid after all.

"This should tell us once and for all if their meat *is* our meat," Hellman said. "This Voozy seems to be the closest thing to a universal drink I've found yet."

"Maybe," Casker said hopefully, "maybe it's just plain water!"

"We'll see." Hellman pried open the lid with the edge of the burner.

Within the vat was a crystal-clear liquid.

"No odor," Casker said, bending over the vat.

The crystal liquid lifted to meet him.

Casker retreated so rapidly that he fell over a box. Hellman helped him to his feet, and they approached the vat again. As they came near, the liquid lifted itself three feet into the air and moved toward them.

"What've you done now?" Casker asked, moving back carefully. The liquid flowed slowly over the side of the vat. It began to flow toward him.

"Hellman!" Casker shrieked.

Hellman was standing to one side, perspiration pouring down his face, reading his dictionary with a preoccupied frown.

"Guess I bumbled the translation," he said.

"Do something!" Casker shouted. The liquid was trying to back him into a corner.

"Nothing I can do," Hellman said, reading on. "Ah, here's the error. It doesn't say 'Everyone drinks Voozy.' Wrong subject. 'Voozy drinks *everyone*.' That tells us something! The Helgans must have soaked liquid in through their pores. Naturally, they would prefer to be drunk, instead of to drink."

Casker tried to dodge around the liquid, but it cut him off with a merry gurgle. Desperately he picked up a small bale and threw it at the Voozy. The Voozy caught the bale and drank it. Then it discarded that and turned back to Casker.

Hellman tossed another box. The Voozy drank this one and a third and fourth that Casker threw in. Then, apparently exhausted, it flowed back into its vat.

Casker clapped down the lid and sat on it, trembling violently.

"Not so good," Hellman said. "We've been taking it for granted that the Helgans had eating habits like us. But, of course, it doesn't necessarily—"

"No, it doesn't. No, sir, it certainly doesn't. I guess we can see that it doesn't. Anyone can see that it doesn't—"

"Stop that," Hellman ordered sternly. "We've no time for hysteria."

"Sorry." Casker slowly moved away from the Voozy vat.

"I guess we'll have to assume that their meat is our poison," Hellman said thoughtfully. "So now we'll see if their poison is our meat."

Casker didn't say anything. He was wondering what would have happened if the Voozy had drunk him.

In the corner, the rubbery block was still giggling to itself.

"Now here's a likely-looking poison," Hellman said, half an hour later.

Casker had recovered completely, except for an occasional twitch of the lips.

"What does it say?" he asked.

Hellman rolled a tiny tube in the palm of his hand. "It's called Pvastkin's Plugger. The label reads: WARNING! HIGHLY DANGEROUS! PVASTKIN'S PLUGGER IS DESIGNED TO FILL HOLES OR CRACKS OF NOT MORE THAN TWO CUBIC VIMS. HOWEVER—THE PLUGGER IS NOT TO BE EATEN UNDER ANY CIRCUMSTANCES. THE ACTIVE INGREDIENT, RAMOTOL, WHICH MAKES PVASTKIN'S SO EXCELLENT A PLUGGER RENDERS IT HIGHLY DANGEROUS WHEN TAKEN INTERNALLY."

"Sounds great," Casker said. "It'll probably blow us sky-high."

"Do you have any other suggestions?" Hellman asked.

Casker thought for a moment. The food of Helg was obviously unpalatable for humans. So perhaps was their poison . . . but wasn't starvation better than this sort of thing?

After a moment's communion with his stomach, he decided that starvation was *not* better.

"Go ahead," he said.

Hellman slipped the burner under his arm and unscrewed the top of the little bottle. He shook it.

Nothing happened.

"It's got a seal," Casker pointed out.

Hellman punctured the seal with his fingernail and set the bottle on the floor. An evil-smelling green froth began to bubble out.

Hellman looked dubiously at the froth. It was congealing into a glob and spreading over the floor.

"Yeast, perhaps," he said, gripping the burner tightly.

"Come, come. Faint heart never filled empty stomach."

"I'm not holding *you* back," Hellman said.

The glob swelled to the size of a man's head.

"How long is that supposed to go on?" Casker asked.

"Well," Hellman said, "it's advertised as a Plugger. I suppose that's what it does—expands to plug up holes."

"Sure. But how *much?*"

"Unfortunately, I don't know how much two cubic vims are. But it can't go on much—"

Belatedly, they noticed that the Plugger had filled almost a quarter of the room and was showing no signs of stopping.

"We should have believed the label!" Casker yelled to him, across the spreading glob. "It *is* dangerous!"

As the Plugger produced more surface, it began to accelerate in its growth. A sticky edge touched Hellman and he jumped back.

"Watch out!"

He couldn't reach Casker, on the other side of the gigantic sphere of blob. Hellman tried to run around, but the Plugger had spread, cutting the room in half. It began to swell toward the walls.

"Run for it!" Hellman yelled, and rushed to the door behind him.

He flung it open just as the expanding glob reached him. On the other side of the room, he heard a door slam shut. Hellman didn't wait any longer. He sprinted through and slammed the door behind him.

He stood for a moment, panting, the burner in his hand. He hadn't realized how weak he was. That sprint had cut his reserves of energy dangerously close to the collapsing point. At least Casker had made it, too, though.

But he was still in trouble.

The Plugger poured merrily through the blasted lock, into the room. Hellman tried a practice shot on it, but the Plugger was evidently impervious . . . as, he realized, a good plugger should be.

It was showing no signs of fatigue.

Hellman hurried to the far wall. The door was locked,

as the others had been, so he burned out the lock and went through.

How far could the glob expand? How much was two cubic vims? Two cubic miles, perhaps? For all he knew, the Plugger was used to repair faults in the crusts of planets.

In the next room, Hellman stopped to catch his breath. He remembered that the building was circular. He would burn his way through the remaining doors and join Casker. They would burn their way outside and . . .

Casker didn't have a burner!

Hellman turned white with shock. Casker had made it into the room on the right, because they had burned it open earlier. The Plugger was undoubtedly oozing into that room, through the shattered lock . . . and Casker couldn't get out! The Plugger was on his left, a locked door on his right!

Rallying his remaining strength, Hellman began to run. Boxes seemed to get in his way purposefully, tripping him, slowing him down. He blasted the next door and hurried on to the next. And the next. And the next.

The Plugger couldn't expand *completely* into Casker's room!

Or could it?

The wedge-shaped rooms, each a segment of a circle, seemed to stretch before him forever, a jumbled montage of locked doors, alien goods, more doors, more goods. Hellman fell over a crate, got to his feet and fell again. He had reached the limit of his strength, and passed it. But Casker was his friend.

Besides, without a pilot, he'd never get off the place.

Hellman struggled through two more rooms on trembling legs and then collapsed in front of a third.

"Is that you, Hellman?" he heard Casker ask, from the other side of the door.

"You all right?" Hellman managed to gasp.

"Haven't much room in here," Casker said, "but the Plugger's stopped growing. Hellman, get me out of here!"

Hellman lay on the floor panting. "Moment," he said.

"Moment, hell!" Casker shouted. "Get me out. I've found water!"

"What? How?"

"Get me out of here!"

Hellman tried to stand up, but his legs weren't co-operating. "What happened?" he asked.

"When I saw that glob filling the room, I figured I'd try to start up the Super Custom Transport. Thought maybe it could knock down the door and get me out. So I pumped it full of high-gain Integor fuel."

"Yes?" Hellman said, still trying to get his legs under control.

"That Super Custom Transport is an animal, Hellman! And the Integor fuel is water! Now get me out!"

Hellman lay back with a contented sigh. If he had had a little more time, he would have worked out the whole thing himself, by pure logic. But it was all very apparent now. The most efficient machine to go over those vertical, razor-sharp mountains would be an animal, probably with retractable suckers. It was kept in hibernation between trips; and if it drank water, the other products designed for it would be palatable, too. Of course they still didn't know much about the late inhabitants, but undoubtedly . . .

"Burn down that door!" Casker shrieked, his voice breaking.

Hellman was pondering the irony of it all. If one man's meat—*and* his poison—are your poison, then try eating something else. So simple, really.

But there was one thing that still bothered him.

"How did you know it was an Earth-type animal?" he asked.

"Its breath, stupid! It inhales and exhales and smells

as if it's eaten onions!" There was a sound of cans falling and bottles shattering. "Now hurry!"

"What's wrong?" Hellman asked, finally getting to his feet and poising the burner.

"The Custom Super Transport. It's got me cornered behind a pile of cases. Hellman, it seems to think that I'm *its* meat!"

THE KING'S WISHES

AFTER SQUATTING behind a glassware display for almost two hours, Bob Granger felt his legs begin to cramp. He moved to ease them, and his number ten iron slipped off his lap, clattering on the floor.

"Shh," Janice whispered, her mashie gripped tightly.

"I don't think he's going to come," Bob said.

"Be quiet, honey," Janice whispered again, peering into the darkness of their store.

There was no sign of the burglar yet. He had come every night in the past week, mysteriously removing generators, refrigerators and air-conditioners. Mysteriously —for he tampered with no locks, jimmied no windows, left no footprints. Yet somehow, he was able to sneak in, time after time, and slink out with a good part of their stock.

"I don't think this was such a good idea," Bob whispered. "After all, a man capable of carrying several hundred pounds of generator on his back—"

"We'll handle him," Janice said, with the certainty that had made her a master sergeant in the WAC Motor

Corps. "Besides, we have to stop him—he's postponing our wedding day."

Bob nodded in the darkness. He and Janice had built and stocked the Country Department Store with their army savings. They were planning on getting married, as soon as the profits enabled them to. But when someone stole refrigerators and air-conditioners—

"I think I hear something," Janice said, shifting her grip on the mashie.

There was a faint noise somewhere in the store. They waited. Then they heard the sound of feet, padding over the linoleum.

"When he gets to the middle of the floor," Janice whispered, "switch on the lights."

Finally they were able to make out a blackness against the lesser blackness of the store. Bob switched on the lights, shouting, "Hold it there!"

"Oh, no!" Janice gasped, almost dropping her mashie. Bob turned and gulped.

Standing in front of them was a being at least ten feet tall. He had budding horns on his forehead, and tiny wings on his back. He was dressed in a pair of dungarees and a white sweatshirt with EBLIS TECH written across it in scarlet letters. Scuffed white buckskins were on his tremendous feet, and he had a blond crewcut.

"Damn," he said, looking at Bob and Janice. "Knew I should have taken Invisibility in college." He wrapped his arms around his stomach and puffed out his cheeks. Instantly his legs disappeared. Puffing out his cheeks still more he was able to make his stomach vanish. But that was as far as it went.

"Can't do it," he said, releasing his stored-up air. His stomach and legs came back into visibility. "Haven't got the knack. Damn."

"What do you want?" Janice asked, drawing herself to her full slender five foot three.

"Want? Let me see. Oh yes. The fan." He walked across the room and picked up a large floor fan.

"Just a minute," Bob shouted. He walked up to the giant, his golf club poised. Janice followed close behind him. "Where do you think you're going with that?"

"To King Alerian," the giant said. "He wished for it."

"Oh, he did, did he?" Janice said. "Better put it down." She poised the mashie over her shoulder.

"But I *can't*," the young giant said, his tiny wings twitching nervously. "It's been wished for."

"You asked for it," Janice said. Although small, she was in fine condition from the WACs, where she had spent her time repairing jeep engines. Now, blond hair flying, she swung her club.

"Ouch!" she said. The mashie bounced off the being's head, almost knocking Janice over with the recoil. At the same time, Bob swung his club at the giant's ribs.

It passed *through* the giant, ricocheting against the floor.

"Force is useless against a ferra," the young giant said apologetically.

"A what?" Bob asked.

"A ferra. We're first cousins of the jinn, and related by marriage to the devas." He started to walk back to the center of the room, the fan gripped in one broad hand. "Now if you'll excuse me—"

"A demon?" Janice stood, open-mouthed. Her parents had allowed no talk of ghosts or demons in the house, and Janice had grown up a hardheaded realist. She was skilled at repairing anything mechanical; that was her part of the partnership. But anything more fanciful she left to Bob.

Bob, having been raised on a liberal feeding of Oz and Burroughs, was more credulous. "You mean you're out of the Arabian Nights?" he asked.

"Oh, no," the ferra said. "The jinn of Arabia are my

cousins, as I said. All demons are related, but I am a ferra, of the ferras."

"Would you mind telling me," Bob asked, "What you are doing with my generator, my air-conditioner, and my refrigerator?"

"I'd be glad to," the ferra said, putting down the fan. He felt around the air, found what he wanted, and sat down on nothingness. Then he crossed his legs and tightened the laces of one buckskin.

"I graduated from Eblis Tech just about three weeks ago," he began. "And of course, I applied for civil service. I come from a long line of government men. Well, the lists were crowded, as they always are, so I—"

"Civil service?" Bob asked.

"Oh, yes. They're all civil service jobs—even the jinni in Aladdin's lamp was a government man. You have to pass the tests, you know."

"Go on," Bob said.

"Well—promise this won't go any farther—I got my job through pull." He blushed orange. "My father is a ferra in the Underworld Council, so he used his influence. I was appointed over 4,000 higher-ranking ferras, to the position of ferra of the King's Cup. That's quite an honor, you know."

There was a short silence. Then the ferra went on.

"I must confess I wasn't ready," he said sadly. "The ferra of the cup has to be skilled in all branches of demonology. I had just graduated from college—with only passing grades. But of course, I thought I could handle anything."

The ferra paused, and rearranged his body more comfortably on the air.

"But I don't want to bother you with my troubles," he said, getting off the air and standing on the floor. "If you'll excuse me—" He picked up the fan.

"Just a minute," Janice said. "Has this king commanded you to get our fan?"

"In a way," the ferra said, turning orange again.

"Well, look," Janice said. "Is this king rich?" She had decided, for the moment, to treat this superstitious entity as a real person.

"He's a very wealthy monarch."

"Then why can't he buy this stuff?" Janice wanted to know. "Why does he have to steal it?"

"Well," the ferra mumbled, "There's no place where he can buy it."

"One of those backward Oriental countries," Janice said, half to herself.

"Why can't he import the goods? Any company would be glad to arrange it."

"This is all very embarrassing," the ferra said, rubbing one buckskin against another. "I wish I could make myself invisible."

"Out with it," Bob said.

"If you must know," the ferra said sullenly, "King Alerian lives in what you would call 2,000 B.C."

"Then how—"

"Oh, just a minute," the young ferra said crossly. "I'll explain everything." He rubbed his perspiring hands on his sweatshirt.

"As I told you, I got the job of ferra of the king's cup. Naturally, I expected the king would ask for jewels or beautiful women, either of which I could have supplied easily. We learn that in first term conjuration. But the king had all the jewels he wanted, and more wives than he knew what to do with. So what does he do but say, 'Ferra, my palace is hot in the summer. Do that which will make my palace cool.'

"I knew right then I was in over my head. It takes an advanced ferra to handle climate. I guess I spent too much time on the track team. I was stuck.

"I hurried to the Master Encyclopedia and looked up Climate. The spells were just too much for me. And of course, I couldn't ask for help. That would have been an admission of incompetence. But I read that there was artificial climate-control in the Twentieth Century. So I walked here, along the narrow trail to the future, and took one of your air-conditioners. When the king wanted me to stop his food from spoiling, I came back for a refrigerator. Then it was—"

"You hooked them all to the generator?" Janice asked, interested in such details.

"Yes. I may not be much with spells, but I'm pretty handy mechanically."

It made sense, Bob thought. After all, who could keep a palace cool in 2,000 B.C.? Not all the money in the world could buy the gust of icy air from an air-conditioner, or the food-saving qualities of a refrigerator. But what still bothered Bob was, what kind of a demon was he? He didn't look Assyrian. Certainly not Egyptian . . .

"No, I don't get it," Janice said. "In the *past?* You mean time travel?"

"Sure. I majored in time travel," the ferra said, with a proud, boyish grin.

Aztec perhaps, Bob thought, although that seemed unlikely. . . .

"Well," Janice said, "why don't you go somewhere else? Why not steal from one of the big department stores?"

"This is the only place the trail to the future leads," the ferra said.

He picked up the fan. "I'm sorry to be doing this, but if I don't make good here, I'll never get another appointment. It'll be limbo for me."

He disappeared.

Half an hour later, Bob and Janice were in a corner booth of an all-night diner, drinking black coffee and talking in low tones.

"I don't believe a word of it," Janice was saying, all her skepticism back in force. "Demons! Ferras!"

"You have to believe it," Bob said wearily. "You saw it."

"I don't have to believe everything I see," Janice said staunchly. Then she thought of the missing articles, the vanishing profits and the increasingly distant marriage. "All right," she said. "Oh, honey, what'll we do?"

"You have to fight magic with magic," Bob said confidently. "He'll be back tomorrow night. We'll be ready for him."

"I'm in favor of that," Janice said. "I know where we can borrow a Winchester—"

Bob shook his head. "Bullets will just bounce off him, or pass through. Good, strong magic, that's what we need. A dose of his own medicine."

"What kind of magic?" Janice asked.

"To play safe," Bob said, "We'd better use all kinds. I wish I knew where he's from. To be really effective, magic—"

"You want more coffee?" the counterman said, appearing suddenly in front of them.

Bob looked up guiltily. Janice blushed.

"Let's go," she said to Bob. "If anyone hears us, we'll be laughed out of town."

They met at the store that evening. Bob had spent the day at the library, gathering his materials. They consisted of 25 sheets covered on both sides with Bob's scrawling script.

"I still wish we had that Winchester," Janice said, picking up a tire iron from the hardware section.

At 11:45 the ferra appeared.

"Hi," he said. "Where do you keep your electric heaters? The king wants something for winter. He's tired of open hearths. Too drafty."

"Begone," Bob said, "in the name of the cross!" He held up a cross.

"Sorry," the ferra said pleasantly. "The ferras aren't connected with Christianity."

"Begone in the name of Namtar and Idpa!" Bob went on, since Mesopotamia was first on his notes. "In the name of Utuq, dweller of the desert, in the name of Telal and Alal—"

"Oh, here they are," the ferra said. "Why do I get myself into these jams? This is the electric model, isn't it? Looks a little shoddy."

"I invoke Rata, the boatbuilder," Bob intoned, switching to Polynesia. "And Hina, the tapa maker."

"Shoddy nothing," Janice said, her business instincts getting the better of her. "That stove is guaranteed for a year. Unconditionally."

"I call on the Heavenly Wolf," Bob went on, moving into China when Polynesia had no effect. "The Wolf who guards the gates of Shang Ti. I invoke the thunder god, Lei Kung—"

"Let's see, I have an infrared broiler," the ferra said. "And I need a bathtub. Have you got a bathtub?"

"I call Bael, Buer, Forcas, Marchocias, Astaroth—"

"These are bathtubs, aren't they?" the ferra asked Janice, who nodded involuntarily. "I think I'll take the largest. The king is a good-sized man."

"—Behemoth, Theutus, Asmodeus and Incubus!" Bob finished. The ferra looked at him with respect.

Angrily Bob invoked Ormazd, Persian king of light, and then the Ammonitic Beelphegor, and Dagon of the ancient Philistines.

"That's all I can carry, I suppose," the ferra said.

Bob invoked Damballa. He called upon the gods of Arabia. He tried Thessalian magic, and spells from Asia Minor. He nudged Aztec gods and stirred Mayan spirits. He tried Africa, Madagascar, India, Ireland, Malaya, Scandinavia and Japan.

"That's impressive," the ferra said, "but it'll really do no good." He lifted the bathtub, broiler and heater.

"Why not?" Bob gasped, out of breath.

"You see, ferras are affected only by their own indigenous spells. Just as Jinn are responsible only to magic laws of Arabia. Also, you don't know my true name, and I assure you, you can't do much of a job of exorcizing anything if you don't know its true name."

"What country are you from?" Bob asked wiping perspiration from his forehead.

"Sorry," the ferra said. "But if you knew that, you might find the right spell to use against me. And I'm in enough trouble as it is."

"Now look," Janice said. "If the king is so rich, why can't he pay?"

"The king never pays for anything he can get free," the ferra said. "That's why he's so rich."

Bob and Janice glared at him, their marriage fading off into the future.

"See you tomorrow night," the ferra said.

He waved a friendy hand, and vanished.

"Well now," Janice said, after the ferra had left. "What now? Any more bright ideas?"

"All out of them," Bob said, sitting down heavily on a sofa.

"Any more magic?" Janice asked, with a faint touch of irony.

"That won't work," Bob said. "I couldn't find *ferra* or *King Alerian* listed in any encyclopedia. He's probably from some place we'd never hear of. A little native state in India, perhaps."

"Just our luck," Janice said, abandoning irony. "What are we going to do? I suppose he'll want a vacuum cleaner next, and then a phonograph." She closed her eyes and concentrated.

"He really is trying to make good," Bob said.

"I think I have an idea," Janice said, opening her eyes.

"What's that?"

"First of all, it's *our* business that's important, and *our* marriage. Right?"

"Right," Bob said.

"All right. I don't know much about spells," Janice said, rolling up her sleeves, "But I do know machines. Let's get to work."

The next night the ferra visited them at a quarter to 11. He wore the same white sweater, but he had exchanged his buckskins for tan loafers.

"The king is in a special rush for this," he said. "His newest wife has been pestering the life out of him. It seems that her clothes last for only one washing. Her slaves beat them with rocks."

"Sure," Bob said.

"Help yourself," Janice said.

"That's awfully decent of you," the ferra said gratefully. "I really appreciate it." He picked up a washing machine. "She's waiting now."

He vanished.

Bob offered Janice a cigarette. They sat down on a couch and waited. In half an hour the ferra appeared again.

"What did you do?" he asked.

"Why, what's the matter?" Janice asked sweetly.

"The washer! When the queen started it, it threw out a great cloud of evil-smelling smoke. Then it made some strange noises and stopped."

"In our language," Janice said, blowing a smoke ring, "we would say it was gimmicked."

"Gimmicked?"

"Rigged. Fixed. Strung. And so's everything else in this place."

"But you can't do that!" the ferra said. "It's not playing the game."

"You're so smart," Janice said venomously, "go ahead and fix it."

"I was boasting," the ferra said in a small voice. "I was much better at sports."

Janice smiled and yawned.

"Well, gee," the ferra said, his little wings twitching nervously.

"Sorry," Bob said.

"This puts me in an awful spot," the ferra said. "I'll be demoted. I'll be thrown out of civil service."

"We can't let ourselves go bankrupt, can we?" Janice asked.

Bob thought for a moment. "Look," he said. "Why don't you tell the king you've met a strong countermagic? Tell him he has to pay a tariff to the demons of the underworld if he wants his stuff."

"He won't like it," the ferra said doubtfully.

"Try it anyhow," Bob suggested.

"I'll try," the ferra said, and vanished.

"How much do you think we can charge?" Janice asked.

"Oh, give him standard rates. After all, we've built this store on fair practices. We wouldn't want to discriminate. I still wish I knew where he was from, though."

"He's so rich," Janice said dreamily. "It seems a shame not to—"

"Wait a minute!" Bob shouted. "We can't do it! How can there be refrigerators in 2,000 before Christ? Or air-conditioners?"

"What do you mean?"

"It would change the whole course of history!" Bob said. "Some smart guy is going to look at those things and figure out how they work. Then the whole course of history will be changed!"

"So what?" Janice asked practically.

"So what? So research will be carried out along different lines. The present will be changed."

"You mean it's impossible?"

"Yes!"

"That's just what I've been saying all along," Janice said triumphantly.

"Oh, stop that," Bob said. "I wish I could figure this out. No matter what country the ferra is from, it's bound to have an effect on the future. We can't have a paradox."

"Why not?" Janice asked, but at that moment the ferra appeared.

"The king has agreed," the ferra said. "Will this pay for what I've taken?" He held out a small sack.

Spilling out the sack, Bob found that it contained about two dozen large rubies, emeralds and diamonds.

"We can't take it," Bob said. "We can't do business with you."

"Don't be superstitious!" Janice shouted, seeing their marriage begin to evaporate again.

"Why not?" the ferra asked.

"We can't introduce modern things into the past," Bob said. "It'll change the present. This world may vanish or something."

"Oh, don't worry about that," the ferra said. "I guarantee nothing will happen."

"But why? I mean, if you introduced a washer in ancient Rome—"

"Unfortunately," the ferra said, "King Alerian's kingdom has no future."

"Would you explain that?"

"Sure." The ferra sat down on the air. "In three years King Alerian and his country will be completely and irrevocably destroyed by forces of nature. Not a person will be saved. Not even a piece of pottery."

"Fine," Janice said, holding a ruby to the light. "We'd better unload while he's still in business."

"I guess that takes care of that," Bob said. Their business was saved, and their marriage was in the immediate future. "How about you?" he asked the ferra.

"Well, I've done rather well on this job," the ferra said.

"I think I'll apply for a foreign transfer. I hear there are some wonderful opportunities in Arabian sorcery."

He ran a hand complacently over his blond crewcut. "I'll be seeing you," he said, and started to disappear.

"Just a minute," Bob said. "Would you mind telling me what country you're from? And what country King Alerian is from?"

"Oh, sure," the ferra said, only his head still visible. "I thought you knew. Ferras are the demons of Atlantis."

And he disappeared.

WARM

ANDERS LAY ON HIS BED, fully dressed except for his shoes and black bow tie, contemplating, with a certain uneasiness, the evening before him. In twenty minutes he would pick up Judy at her apartment, and that was the uneasy part of it.

He had realized, only seconds ago, that he was in love with her.

Well, he'd tell her. The evening would be memorable. He would propose, there would be kisses, and the seal of acceptance would, figuratively speaking, be stamped across his forehead.

Not too pleasant an outlook, he decided. It really would be much more comfortable not to be in love. What had done it? A look, a touch, a thought? It didn't take much, he knew, and stretched his arms for a thorough yawn.

"Help me!" a voice said.

His muscles spasmed, cutting off the yawn in mid-moment. He sat upright on the bed, then grinned and lay back again.

"You must help me!" the voice insisted.

Anders sat up, reached for a polished shoe and fitted it on, giving his full attention to the tying of the laces.

"Can you hear me?" the voice asked. "You can, can't you?"

That did it. "Yes, I can hear you," Anders said, still in a high good humor. "Don't tell me you're my guilty subconscious, attacking me for a childhood trauma I never bothered to resolve. I suppose you want me to join a monastery."

"I don't know what you're talking about," the voice said. "I'm no one's subconscious. I'm *me*. Will you help me?"

Anders believed in voices as much as anyone; that is, he didn't believe in them at all, until he heard them. Swiftly he catalogued the possibilities. Schizophrenia was the best answer, of course, and one in which his colleagues would concur. But Anders had a lamentable confidence in his own sanity. In which case—

"Who are you?" he asked.

"I don't know," the voice answered.

Anders realized that the voice was speaking within his own mind. Very suspicious.

"You don't know who you are," Anders stated. "Very well. *Where* are you?"

"I don't know that, either." The voice paused, and went on. "Look, I know how ridiculous this must sound. Believe me, I'm in some sort of limbo. I don't know how I got here or who I am, but I want desperately to get out. Will you help me?"

Still fighting the idea of a voice speaking within his head, Anders knew that his next decision was vital. He had to accept—or reject—his own sanity.

He accepted it.

"All right," Anders said, lacing the other shoe. "I'll grant that you're a person in trouble, and that you're in

some sort of telepathic contact with me. Is there anything else you can tell me?"

"I'm afraid not," the voice said, with infinite sadness.
"You'll have to find out for yourself."

"Can you contact anyone else?"

"No."

"Then how can you talk with me?"

"I don't know."

Anders walked to his bureau mirror and adjusted his
black bow tie, whistling softly under his breath. Having
just discovered that he was in love, he wasn't going to
let a little thing like a voice in his mind disturb him.

"I really don't see how I can be of any help," Anders
said, brushing a bit of lint from his jacket. "You don't
know where you are, and there don't seem to be any
distinguishing landmarks. How am I to find you?" He
turned and looked around the room to see if he had forgotten anything.

"I'll know when you're close," the voice said. "You
were warm just then."

"Just then?" All he had done was look around the
room. He did so again, turning his head slowly. Then it
happened.

The room, from one angle, looked different. It was
suddenly a mixture of muddled colors, instead of the carefully blended pastel shades he had selected. The lines of
wall, floor and ceiling were strangely off proportion, zig-
zag, unrelated.

Then everything went back to normal.

"You were *very* warm," the voice said.

Anders resisted the urge to scratch his head, for fear of
disarranging his carefully combed hair. What he had seen
wasn't so strange. Everyone sees one or two things in his
life that make him doubt his normality, doubt sanity,
doubt his very existence. For a moment the orderly Universe is disarranged and the fabric of belief is ripped.

But the moment passes.

Anders remembered once, as a boy, awakening in his room in the middle of the night. How strange everything had looked! Chairs, table, all out of proportion, swollen in the dark. The ceiling pressing down, as in a dream.

But that also had passed.

"Well, old man," he said, "if I get warm again, tell me."

"I will," the voice in his head whispered. "I'm sure you'll find me."

"I'm glad you're so sure," Anders said gaily, switched off the lights and left.

Lovely and smiling, Judy greeted him at the door. Looking at her, Anders sensed her knowledge of the moment. Had she felt the change in him, or predicted it? Or was love making him grin like an idiot?

"Would you like a before-party drink?" she asked.

He nodded, and she led him across the room, to the improbable green-and-yellow couch. Sitting down, Anders decided he would tell her when she came back with the drink. No use in putting off the fatal moment. A lemming in love, he told himself.

"You're getting warm again," the voice said.

He had almost forgotten his invisible friend. Or fiend, as the case could well be. What would Judy say if she knew he was hearing voices? Little things like that, he reminded himself, often break up the best of romances.

"Here," she said, handing him a drink.

Still smiling, he noticed. The number two smile—to a prospective suitor, provocative and understanding. It had been preceded, in their relationship, by the number one nice-girl smile, the don't-misunderstand-me smile, to be worn on all occasions, until the correct words have been mumbled.

"That's right," the voice said. "It's in how you look at things."

Look at what? Anders glanced at Judy, annoyed at his thoughts. If he was going to play the lover, let him play it. Even through the astigmatic haze of love, he was able to appreciate her blue-gray eyes, her fine skin (if one overlooked a tiny blemish on the left temple) , her lips, slightly reshaped by lipstick.

"How did your classes go today?" she asked.

Well, of course she'd ask that, Anders thought. Love is marking time.

"All right," he said. "Teaching psychology to young apes—"

"Oh, come now!"

"Warmer," the voice said.

What's the matter with me, Anders wondered. She really is a lovely girl. The *gestalt* that is Judy, a pattern of thoughts, expressions, movements, making up the girl I—

I what?

Love?

Anders shifted his long body uncertainly on the couch. He didn't quite understand how this train of thought had begun. It annoyed him. The analytical young instructor was better off in the classroom. Couldn't science wait until 9:10 in the morning?

"I was thinking about you today," Judy said, and Anders knew that she had sensed the change in his mood.

"Do you see?" the voice asked him. "You're getting much better at it."

"I don't see anything," Anders thought, but the voice was right. It was as though he had a clear line of inspection into Judy's mind. Her feelings were nakedly apparent to him, as meaningless as his room had been in that flash of undistorted thought.

"I really was thinking about you," she repeated.

"Now look," the voice said.

Anders, watching the expressions on Judy's face, felt the strangeness descend on him. He was back in the nightmare perception of that moment in his room. This time it was as though he were watching a machine in a laboratory. The object of this operation was the evocation and preservation of a particular mood. The machine goes through a searching process, invoking trains of ideas to achieve the desired end.

"Oh, were you?" he asked, amazed at his new perspective.

"Yes . . . I wondered what you were doing at noon," the reactive machine opposite him on the couch said, expanding its shapely chest slightly.

"Good," the voice said, commending him for his perception.

"Dreaming of you, of course," he said to the flesh-clad skeleton behind the total *gestalt* Judy. The flesh machine rearranged its limbs, widened its mouth to denote pleasure. The mechanism searched through a complex of fears, hopes, worries, through half-remembrances of analogous situations, analogous solutions.

And this was what he loved. Anders saw too clearly and hated himself for seeing. Through his new nightmare perception, the absurdity of the entire room struck him.

"Were you really?" the articulating skeleton asked him.

"You're coming closer," the voice whispered.

To what? The personality? There was no such thing. There was no true cohesion, no depth, nothing except a web of surface reactions, stretched across automatic visceral movements.

He was coming closer to the truth.

"Sure," he said sourly.

The machine stirred, searching for a response.

Anders felt a quick tremor of fear at the sheer alien quality of his viewpoint. His sense of formalism had been sloughed off, his agreed-upon reactions by-passed. What would be revealed next?

He was seeing clearly, he realized, as perhaps no man had ever seen before. It was an oddly exhilarating thought.

But could he still return to normality?

"Can I get you a drink?" the reaction machine asked.

At that moment Anders was as thoroughly out of love as a man could be. Viewing one's intended as a depersonalized, sexless piece of machinery is not especially conducive to love. But it is quite stimulating, intellectually.

Anders didn't want normality. A curtain was being raised and he wanted to see behind it. What was it some Russian scientist—Ouspensky, wasn't it—had said?

"Think in other categories."

That was what he was doing, and would continue to do.

"Good-by," he said suddenly.

The machine watched him, open-mouthed, as he walked out the door. Delayed circuit reactions kept it silent until it heard the elevator door close.

"You were very warm in there," the voice within his head whispered, once he was on the street. "But you still don't understand everything."

"Tell me, then," Anders said, marveling a little at his equanimity. In an hour he had bridged the gap to a completely different viewpoint, yet it seemed perfectly natural.

"I can't," the voice said. "You must find it yourself."

"Well, let's see now," Anders began. He looked around at the masses of masonry, the convention of streets cutting through the architectural piles. "Human life," he said, "is a series of conventions. When you look at a girl, you're supposed to see—a pattern, not the underlying formlessness."

"That's true," the voice agreed, but with a shade of doubt.

"Basically, there is no form. Man produces *gestalts*, and cuts form out of the plethora of nothingness. It's like looking at a set of lines and saying that they represent a figure. We look at a mass of material, extract it from the background and say it's a man. But in truth, there is no such thing. There are only the humanizing features that we—myopically—attach to it. Matter is conjoined, a matter of viewpoint."

"You're not seeing it now," said the voice.

"Damn it," Anders said. He was certain that he was on the track of something big, perhaps something ultimate. "Everyone's had the experience. At some time in his life, everyone looks at a familiar object and can't make any sense out of it. Momentarily, the *gestalt* fails, but the true moment of sight passes. The mind reverts to the superimposed pattern. Normalcy continues."

The voice was silent. Anders walked on, through the *gestalt* city.

"There's something else, isn't there?" Anders asked.

"Yes."

What could that be, he asked himself. Through clearing eyes, Anders looked at the formality he had called his world.

He wondered momentarily if he would have come to this if the voice hadn't guided him. Yes, he decided after a few moments, it was inevitable.

But who was the voice? And what had he left out?

"Let's see what a party looks like now," he said to the voice.

The party was a masquerade; the guests were all wearing their faces. To Anders, their motives, individually and collectively, were painfully apparent. Then his vision began to clear further.

He saw that the people weren't truly individual. They were discontinuous lumps of flesh sharing a common vocabulary, yet not even truly discontinuous.

The lumps of flesh were a part of the decoration of the room and almost indistinguishable from it. They were one with the lights, which lent their tiny vision. They were joined to the sounds they made, a few feeble tones out of the great possibility of sound. They blended into the walls.

The kaleidoscopic view came so fast that Anders had

trouble sorting his new impressions. He knew now that these people existed only as patterns, on the same basis as the sounds they made and the things they thought they saw.

Gestalts, sifted out of the vast, unbearable real world.

"Where's Judy?" a discontinuous lump of flesh asked him. This particular lump possessed enough nervous mannerisms to convince the other lumps of his reality. He wore a loud tie as further evidence.

"She's sick," Anders said. The flesh quivered into an instant sympathy. Lines of formal mirth shifted to formal woe.

"Hope it isn't anything serious," the vocal flesh remarked.

"You're warmer," the voice said to Anders.

Anders looked at the object in front of him.

"She hasn't long to live," he stated.

The flesh quivered. Stomach and intestines contracted in sympathetic fear. Eyes distended, mouth quivered.

The loud tie remained the same.

"My God! you don't mean it!"

"What are you?" Anders asked quietly.

"What do you mean?" the indignant flesh attached to the tie demanded. Serene within its reality, it gaped at Anders. Its mouth twitched, undeniable proof that it was real and sufficient. "You're drunk," it sneered.

Anders laughed and left the party.

"There is still something you don't know," the voice said. "But you were hot! I could feel you near me."

"What are you?" Anders asked again.

"I don't know," the voice admitted. "I am a person. I am I. I am trapped."

"So are we all," Anders said. He walked on asphalt, surrounded by heaps of concrete, silicates, aluminum and iron alloys. Shapeless, meaningless heaps that made up the *gestalt* city.

And then there were the imaginary lines of demarcation dividing city from city, the artificial boundaries of water and land.

All ridiculous.

"Give me a dime for some coffee, mister?" something asked, a thing indistinguishable from any other thing.

"Old Bishop Berkeley would give a nonexistent dime to your nonexistent presence," Anders said gaily.

"I'm really in a bad way," the voice whined, and Anders perceived that it was no more than a series of modulated vibrations.

"Yes! Go on!" the voice commanded.

"If you could spare me a quarter—" the vibrations said, with a deep pretense at meaning.

No, what was there behind the senseless patterns? Flesh, mass. What was that? All made up of atoms.

"I'm really hungry," the intricately arranged atoms muttered.

All atoms. Conjoined. There were no true separations between atom and atom. Flesh was stone, stone was light. Anders looked at the masses of atoms that were pretending to solidity, meaning and reason.

"Can't you help me?" a clump of atoms asked. But the clump was identical with all the other atoms. Once you ignored the superimposed patterns, you could see the atoms were random, scattered.

"I don't believe in you," Anders said.

The pile of atoms was gone.

"Yes!" the voice cried. "Yes!"

"I don't believe in any of it," Anders said. After all, what was an atom?

"Go on!" the voice shouted. "You're hot! Go on!"

What was an atom? An empty space surrounded by an empty space.

Absurd!

"Then it's all false!" Anders said. And he was alone under the stars.

"That's right!" the voice within his head screamed. "Nothing!"

But stars, Anders thought. How can one believe—

The stars disappeared. Anders was in a gray nothingness, a void. There was nothing around him except shapeless gray.

Where was the voice?

Gone.

Anders perceived the delusion behind the grayness, and then there was nothing at all.

Complete nothingness, and himself within it.

Where was he? What did it mean? Anders' mind tried to add it up.

Impossible. *That* couldn't be true.

Again the score was tabulated, but Anders' mind couldn't accept the total. In desperation, the overloaded mind erased the figures, eradicated the knowledge, erased itself.

"Where am I?"

In nothingness. Alone.

Trapped.

"Who am I?"

A voice.

The voice of Anders searched the nothingness, shouted, "Is there anyone here?"

No answer.

But there was someone. All directions were the same, yet moving along one he could make contact . . . with someone. The voice of Anders reached back to someone who could save him, perhaps.

"Save me," the voice said to Anders, lying fully dressed on his bed, except for his shoes and black bow tie.

THE DEMONS

WALKING ALONG SECOND AVENUE, Arthur Gammet decided it was a rather nice spring day. Not too cold, just brisk and invigorating. A perfect day for selling insurance, he told himself. He stepped off the curb at Ninth Street.

And vanished.

"Didja see that?" A butcher's assistant asked the butcher. They had been standing in front of their store, idly watching people go by.

"See what?" the butcher, a corpulent, red-faced man, replied.

"The guy in the overcoat. He disappeared."

"Yeh," the butcher said. "So he turned up Ninth, so what?"

The butcher's assistant hadn't seen Arthur turn up Ninth, down Ninth, or across Second. He had seen him disappear. But should he insist on it? You tell your boss he's wrong, so where does it get you? Besides, the guy in the overcoat probably *had* turned up Ninth. Where else could he have gone?

But Arthur Gammet was no longer in New York. He had thoroughly vanished.

Somewhere else, not necessarily on Earth, a being who called himself Neelsebub was staring at a pentagon. Within it was something he hadn't bargained for. Neelsebub fixed it with a bitter stare, knowing he had good cause for anger. He'd spent years digging out magic formulas, experimenting with herbs and essences, reading the best books on wizardry and witchcraft. He'd thrown every-

108

thing into one gigantic effort, and what happened? The wrong demon appeared.

Of course, there were many things that might have gone amiss. The severed hand of the corpse—it just *might* have been the hand of a suicide, for even the best of dealers aren't to be trusted. Or the line of the pentagon might have been the least bit wavy; that was very significant. Or the words of the incantation might not have been in the proper order. Even one syllable wrongly intoned could have done it.

Anyhow, the damage was done. Neelsebub leaned one red-scaled shoulder against the huge bottle in back of him, scratching the other shoulder with a dagger-like fingernail. As usual when perplexed, his barbed tail flicked uncertainly.

At least he had a demon of some sort.

But the thing inside the pentagon didn't look like any conventional kind of demon. Those loose folds of gray flesh, for example . . . But then, the historical accounts were notoriously inaccurate. Whatever kind of supernatural being it was, it would have to come across. Of that he was certain. Neelsebub folded his hooved feet under him more comfortably, waiting for the strange being to speak.

Arthur Gammet was still too stunned to speak. One moment he had been walking to the insurance office, minding his own business, enjoying the fine air of an early spring morning. He had stepped off the curb at Second and Ninth—and landed here. Wherever *here* was.

Swaying slightly, he made out, through the deep mist that filled the room, a huge red-scaled monster squatting on its haunches. Beside it was what looked like a bottle, but a bottle fully ten feet high. The creature had a barbed tail and was now scratching his head with it, glaring at Arthur out of little piggish eyes. Hastily, Arthur tried to step back, but was unable to move more than a step. He was inside a chalked area, he noticed, and for some reason was unable to step over the white lines.

"So," the red creature said, finally breaking the silence. "I've finally got you." These weren't the words he was saying; the sounds were utterly foreign. But somehow, Arthur was able to understand the thought behind the words. It wasn't telepathy, but rather as though he were translating a foreign language, automatically, colloquially.

"I must say I'm rather disappointed," Neelsebub continued when the captured demon in the pentagon didn't answer. "All our legends say that demons are fearful things, fifteen feet high, with wings and tiny heads and a hole in the chest that throws out jets of cold water."

Arthur Gammet peeled off his overcoat, letting it fall in a sodden heap at his feet. Dimly, he could appreciate the idea of demons being able to produce jets of cold water. The room was like a furnace. Already his gray tweed suit was a soggy, wrinkled mass of cloth and perspiration.

And with that thought came acceptance—of the red creature, the chalk lines he was unable to cross, the sweltering room—everything.

He had noticed in books, magazine and motion-pictures that a man, confronted by an odd situation, usually mouthed lines such as, "Pinch me, this can't be true," or, "Good God, I'm either dreaming, drunk or crazy." Arthur had no intention of saying anything so palpably absurd. For one thing, he was sure the huge red creature wouldn't appreciate it; and for another, he knew he wasn't dreaming, drunk or crazy. There were no words in Arthur Gammet's vocabulary for it, but he knew. A dream was one thing; this was another.

"The legends never mentioned being able to peel off your skin," Neelsebub said thoughtfully, looking at the overcoat at Arthur's feet. "Interesting."

"This is a mistake," Arthur said firmly. The experience he had had as an insurance agent stood him in good stead now. He was used to meeting all kinds of people, unraveling all kinds of snarled situations. This creature had, evidently, tried to raise a demon. Through nobody's fault he had gotten Arthur Gammet, and was under the impression that *he* was a demon. The error must be rectified at once.

"I am an insurance agent," he said. The creature shook its tremendous horned head. Its tail swished from side to side unpleasantly.

"Your other-world functions don't concern me in the slightest," Neelsebub growled. "I don't care, really, what species of demon you are."

"But I tell you I'm not a—"

"It won't work!" Neelsebub howled, glaring angrily at Arthur from the edge of the pentagon. "I know you're a demon. And I want *drast!*"

"Drast? I don't think—"

"I'm up to all your demoniac tricks," Neelsebub said, calming himself with obvious effort. "I know—and you know—that when a demon is conjured, he must grant one wish. I conjured you, and I want drast. Ten thousand pounds of it."

"Drast . . ." Arthur began uncomfortably, standing in the corner of the pentagon furthest from the tail-lashing monster.

"Drast, or voot, or hakatinny, or sup-der-oop. It's all the same thing."

It was speaking of money, Arthur Gammet realized. The slang terms had been unfamiliar, but there was no mistaking the sense behind them. Undoubtedly, drast was what passed for currency in its country.

"Ten thousand pounds isn't much," Neelsebub said with a cunning little smile. "Not for *you*. You ought to be glad I'm not one of those fools who ask for immortality."

Arthur was.

"And if I don't?" he asked.

"In that case," Neelsebub replied, a frown replacing the little smile, "I'll be forced to conjure you again—inside the bottle." Arthur looked at the green bottle, towering over Neelsebub's head. It was wide at its misty base, tapering to a slim neck. If the thing ever got him in, he would never be able to squeeze out through that neck. *If* the thing could get him in. And Arthur was fairly sure it could.

"Of course," Neelsebub said, his smile returning, more cunning than ever, "There's no reason for heroic measures. Ten thousand pounds of the old sup-der-oop isn't much for you. It'll make me rich, but all you have to do is wave your hand." He paused, his smile becoming ingratiating.

"You know," he went on softly, "I've really spent a long time on this. Read a lot of books, spent a pile of voot." His tail lashed the floor suddenly, like a bullet glancing off granite. "Don't try to put something over on me!" he shouted.

Arthur found that the force rising from the chalk extended as high as he could reach. Gingerly, he leaned against the invisible wall, and, finding that it supported his weight, rested against it.

Ten thousand pounds of drast, he thought. Evidently the creature was a sorcerer, from God-knows-where. Some other planet, perhaps. The creature had tried to conjure a wish-granting demon, and had gotten him. It wanted something from him—or else the bottle. All very unreasonable, but Arthur Gammet was beginning to suspect that most wizards were unreasonable people.

"I'll try to get your drast," Arthur said, feeling that he had to say something. "But I'll have to go back to the —ah—underworld to get it. That handwaving stuff is out."

"All right," the monster said to him, standing at the

edge of the pentagon and leering in. "I trust you. But remember, I can call you any time I want. You can't get away, you know, so don't even try. By the way, my name is Neelsebub."

"Any relation to Beelzebub?" Arthur asked.

"Great-grandfather," Neelsebub replied, looking suspiciously at Arthur. "He was an army man. Unfortunately, he—" Neelsebub stopped abruptly, glaring angrily at Arthur. "But you demons know all about that! Begone! *And bring that drast!*"

Arthur Gammet vanished again.

He materialized on the corner of Second Avenue and Ninth Street, where he had first vanished. His overcoat was at his feet, his clothes filled with perspiration. He staggered for a moment to hold his balance—since he had been leaning against the wall of force when Neelsebub had vanished him—picked up his overcoat and hurried to his apartment. Luckily, there had been only a few people around. Two housewives gulped and walked quickly away. A nattily dressed man blinked four or five times, took a step forward as though he wanted to ask something, changed his mind and hurried off toward Eighth Street. The rest of the people either hadn't seen him or just didn't give a damn.

In his two-room apartment Arthur made one feeble attempt to dismiss the whole thing as a dream. Failing miserably, he began to outline his possibilities.

He could produce the drast. That is, perhaps he could if he found out what it was. The stuff Neelsebub considered valuable might be just about anything. Lead, perhaps, or iron. Even that would stretch his meagre earnings to the breaking-point.

He could notify the police. And be locked up in an asylum. Forget that one.

Or, he could not produce the drast—and spend the rest of his life in a bottle. Forget that one, too.

All he could do was wait until Neelsebub conjured him again, and find out then what drast was. Perhaps it was common dirt. He could get that from his uncle's farm in New Jersey, if Neelsebub could manage the transportation.

Arthur Gammet telephoned the office and told them he was ill, and that he expected to be ill for several days. After that he fixed a bite of food in his kitchenette, feeling quite proud of his good appetite. Not everyone faced with the strong possibilty of being shut up in a bottle could have tucked away a meal that well. He tidied up the place, and changed into a light Palm Beach suit. It was four-thirty in the afternoon. He stretched out on the bed and waited. Along about nine-thirty he disappeared.

"Changed your skin again," Neelsebub commented. "Where's the drast?" His tail twitched eagerly as he hurried around the pentagon.

"It's not hidden behind me," Arthur said, turning to look at Neelsebub. "I'll have to have more information." He adopted a nonchalant pose, leaning against the invisible lines that radiated from the chalk. "And I'll have to have your promise that once I produce it you'll leave me alone."

"Of course," Neelsebub answered cheerfully. "I can only ask for one wish anyhow. Tell you what, I'll swear the great oath of Satanas. That's absolutely binding, you know."

"Satanas?"

"One of our early presidents," Neelsebub said with a reverential air. "My great grandfather Beelzebub served under him. Unfortunately—oh, well, you know all that."

Neelsebub swore the great oath of Satanas, and very impressive it was. The blue mists in the room were edged in red when he was done, and the outlines of the huge bottle shifted eerily in the dim light. Arthur was perspiring freely, even in his summer suit. He wished he were a cold-producing demon.

"That's it," Neelsebub said, standing erectly in the middle of the room, his tail looped around his wrist. There was a strange look in his eyes, a look of one re-calling past glories.

"Now what sort of information do you want?" Neelse-bub began pacing the floor in front of the pentagon, his tail dragging.

"Describe this drast to me."

"Well, it's soft, heavy—"

That could be lead.

"And yellow."

Gold.

"Hmm," Arthur said, staring at the bottle. "I don't suppose it's ever gray, is it? Or dark brown?"

"No. It's always yellow. With sometimes a reddish hue."

Still gold. Arthur contemplated the red-scaled mon-ster in front of him, pacing up and down with ill-con-cealed eagerness. Ten thousand pounds of gold. That would come to . . . No, better not think of it. Impos-sible.

"I'll need a little time," Arthur said. "Perhaps sixty or seventy years. Tell you what, I'll call you as soon as—"

Neelsebub interrupted him with a huge roar of laugh-ter. Arthur had tickled his rudimentary sense of humor, evidently, because Neelsebub was hugging his haunches, screaming with mirth.

"Sixty or seventy years!" Neelsebub shouted, and the bottle shook, and even the lines of the pentagon seemed to waver. "I'll give you sixty or seventy minutes! Or the bottle!"

"Now just a minute," Arthur said, from the far side of the pentagon. "I'll need a little—hold it!" He had just had an idea, and it was undeniably the best idea he had ever had. More, it was his own idea.

"I'll have to have the exact formula you used to get me," Arthur said. "Must check with the main office to be sure everything is in order."

The monster raved and swore, and the air turned black and purple; the bottle rang in sympathetic vibration with Neelsebub's voice, and the very room seemed to sway. But Arthur Gammet stood firm. He explained to Neelsebub, patiently, seven or eight times, that it would do no good to bottle him, since he would never get his gold that way. All he wanted was the formula, and certainly that wouldn't—

Finally he got it.

"And no tricks!" Neelsebub thundered finally, gesturing at the bottle with both hands and his tail. Arthur nodded feebly and reappeared in his room.

The next few days he spent in a frenzied search around New York. Some of the ingredients of the incantation were easy to fill—the sprig of mistletoe, for example, from a florist, and the sulphur. Graveyard mold was more difficult, as was a bat's left wing. What really had him stumped for a while was the severed hand of the murdered man. He finally procured one from a store that specialized in filling orders for medical students. He had the dealer's guarantee that the body to which the hand belonged had died a violent death. Arthur suspected that the dealer was trying to humor him, but there was really very little he could do about it.

Among other things, he bought a large bottle. It was surprisingly inexpensive. There were really compensations for living in New York, he decided. There seemed to be nothing—literally *nothing* one couldn't buy.

In three days he had all his materials, and at midnight of the third night he arranged them on the floor of his apartment. The light of a three-quarters full moon was shining in the window—the incantation had been vague as to what phase it should be—and everything seemed to be in order. Arthur drew the pentagon, lighted the candles, burned the incense, and started the chant. He figured that, by following directions carefully, he should be able to conjure Neelsebub. His one wish would be that Neelsebub leave him strictly alone. He couldn't see how that would fail.

The blue mists spread through the room as he mumbled the formula, and soon he could see something growing in the center of the pentagon.

"Neelsebub!" he cried. But it wasn't.

The thing in the pentagon was about fifteen feet high when the incantation was finished. It had to stoop almost to the ground to fit under Arthur's ceiling. It was a fearful-looking thing, with wings and a tiny head and a hole in its chest.

Arthur Gammet had conjured the wrong demon.

"What's all this?" the demon asked, shooting a jet of ice water out of his chest. The water splashed against the invisible walls of the pentagon and rolled to the floor. It must have been pure reflex, because Arthur's room was pleasantly cool.

"I want my one wish," Arthur said. The demon was blue and impossibly thin; his wings were vestigial stumps. They flapped once or twice against his bony chest before he answered.

"I don't know what you are or how you got me here," the demon said. "But it's clever. It's undeniably clever."

"Let's not chatter," Arthur replied nervously, wondering how soon Neelsebub was going to conjure him again. "I want ten thousand pounds of gold. Also known as drast, hakatinny, and the old sup-der-oop." At any moment, he thought, he might find himself inside a bottle.

"Well," the cold-producing demon said. "You seem to be laboring under the mistaken impression that I'm—"

"You have twenty-four hours."

"I'm not a rich man," the cold-producing demon said.

"Small businessman. But perhaps if you give me time—"

"Or the bottle," Arthur said. He pointed to the large bottle in one corner, then realized it would never hold fifteen feet of cold-producing demon.

"The next time I conjure you I'll have a bottle big enough," Arthur said. "I didn't think you'd be so tall."

"We have stories about people disappearing," the demon mused. "So *this* is what happens to them. The underworld. Don't suppose anyone would believe me, though."

"Get that drast," Arthur said. "Begone!"

The cold-producing demon was gone.

Arthur Gammet knew he could not afford more than twenty-four hours. Even that was probably cutting it too thin, he thought, because one could never tell when Neelsebub would decide he had had enough time. There was no telling what the red-scaled monster would do, if he were disappointed a third time. Arthur found that, toward the end of the day, he was clutching the steam pipe. A lot of good that would do if he were conjured! But it was nice to have something solid to grasp.

It was a shame also, he thought, to have to impose on the cold-producing demon that way. It was pretty obvious that the demon wasn't a real demon, any more than Arthur was. Well, he would never use the bottle on him. It would do no good if Neelsebub weren't satisfied.

Finally he mumbled the incantation again.

"You'll have to make your pentagon wider," the cold-producing demon said, stooping uncomfortably inside. "I haven't got room for—"

"Begone!" Arthur said, and feverishly rubbed out the pentagon. He sketched it again, this time using the area of the whole rom. He lugged the bottle—the same one, since he hadn't found one fifteen feet high—into the kitchen, stationed himself in the closet, and went through the formula again. Once more the thick, twisting blue mists gathered.

"Now don't be hasty," the cold-producing demon said, from within the pentagon. "I haven't got the old sup-der-oop yet. There's a tie-up, and I can explain everything." He beat his wings to part the mist. Beside him was a bottle, fully ten feet high. Within it, green with rage, was Neelsebub. He seemed to be shouting, but the bottle was stoppered. No sound came through.

"Got the formula out of the library," the demon said, "Could have knocked me over when the thing worked. Always been a hard-headed businessman, you know. Don't like this supernatural stuff. But, you have to face facts. Anyhow, I got hold of this demon here—" He jerked a spidery arm at the bottle— "But he wouldn't come across. So I bottled him." The cold-producing demon heaved a deep sigh when Arthur smiled. It was like a reprieve.

"Now, I don't want you to bottle me," the cold-producing demon went on, "because I've got a wife and three kids. You know how it is. Insurance slump and all that, I couldn't raise ten thousand pounds of drast with an army. But as soon as I persuade this demon here—"

"Never mind about the drast," Arthur said. "Just take the demon with you. Keep him in storage. Inside the bottle, of course."

"I'll do that," the blue-winged insurance man said. "And about that drast—"

"Forget it," Arthur said warmly. After all, insurance men have to stick together. "Handle fire and theft?"

"General accident is more my line," the insurance man said. "But you know, I've been thinking—"

Neelsebub raved and swore inside the bottle while the two insurance men discussed the intricacies of their profession.

SPECIALIST

THE PHOTON STORM struck without warning, pouncing upon the Ship from behind a bank of giant red stars. Eye barely had time to flash a last second warning through Talker before it was upon them.

It was Talker's third journey into deep space, and his first light-pressure storm. He felt a sudden pang of fear as the Ship yawed violently, caught the force of the wave-front and careened end for end. Then the fear was gone, replaced by a strong pulse of excitement.

Why should he be afraid, he asked himself—hadn't he been trained for just this sort of emergency?

He had been talking to Feeder when the storm hit, but he cut off the conversation abruptly. He hoped Feeder would be all right. It was the youngster's first deep space trip.

The wirelike filaments that made up most of Talker's body were extended throughout the Ship. Quickly he withdrew all except the ones linking him to Eye, Engine, and the Walls. This was strictly their job now. The rest of the Crew would have to shift for themselves until the storm was over.

Eye had flattened his disklike body against a Wall, and had one seeing organ extended outside the Ship. For greater concentration, the rest of his seeing organs were collapsed, clustered against his body.

Through Eye's seeing organ, Talker watched the storm. He translated Eye's purely visual image into a direction for Engine, who shoved the Ship around to meet the waves. At appreciably the same time, Talker translated direction into velocity for the Walls who stiffened to meet the shocks.

The coordination was swift and sure—Eye measuring the waves, Talker relaying the messages to Engine and Walls, Engine driving the ship nose-first into the waves, and Walls bracing to meet the shock.

Talker forgot any fear he might have had in the swiftly functioning teamwork. He had no time to think. As the Ship's communication system, he had to translate and flash his messages at top speed, coordinating information and directing action.

In a matter of minutes, the storm was over.

"All right," Talker said. "Let's see if there was any damage." His filaments had become tangled during the storm, but he untwisted and extended them through the Ship, plugging everyone into circuit. "Engine?"

"I'm fine," Engine said. The tremendous old fellow had dampened his plates during the storm, easing down the atomic explosions in his stomach. No storm could catch an experienced spacer like Engine unaware.

"Walls?"

The Walls reported one by one, and this took a long time. There were almost a thousand of them, thin, rectangular fellows making up the entire skin of the Ship. Naturally, they had reinforced their edges during the storm, giving the whole Ship resiliency. But one or two were dented badly.

Doctor announced that he was all right. He removed Talker's filament from his head, taking himself out of circuit, and went to work on the dented Walls. Made mostly of hands, Doctor had clung to an Accumulator during the storm.

"Let's go a little faster now," Talker said, remembering that there still was the problem of determining where they were. He opened the circuit to the four Accumulators. "How are you?" he asked.

There was no answer. The Accumulators were asleep. They had had their receptors open during the storm and were bloated on energy. Talker twitched his filaments around them, but they didn't stir.

"Let me," Feeder said. Feeder had taken quite a beating before planting his suction cups to a Wall, but his cockiness was intact. He was the only member of the Crew who never needed Doctor's attention; his body was quite capable of repairing itself.

He scuttled across the floor on a dozen or so tentacles, and booted the nearest Accumulator. The big, conial storage unit opened one eye, then closed it again. Feeder kicked him again, getting no response. He reached for the Accumulator's safety valve and drained off some energy.

"Stop that," the Accumulator said.

"Then wake up and report," Talker told him.

The Accumulators said testily that they were all right, as any fool could see. They had been anchored to the floor during the storm.

The rest of the inspection went quickly. Thinker was fine, and Eye was ecstatic over the beauty of the storm. There was only one casualty.

Pusher was dead. Bipedal, he didn't have the stability of the rest of the Crew. The storm had caught him in the middle of a floor, thrown him against a stiffened Wall, and broken several of his important bones. He was beyond Doctor's skill to repair.

They were silent for a while. It was always serious when a part of the Ship died. The Ship was a cooperative unit, composed entirely of the Crew. The loss of any member was a blow to all the rest.

It was especially serious now. They had just delivered a cargo to a port several thousand light-years from Galactic Center. There was no telling where they might be.

Eye crawled to a Wall and extended a seeing organ out-

side. The Walls let it through, then sealed around it.
Eye's organ pushed out, far enough from the Ship so he
could view the entire sphere of stars. The picture traveled
through Talker, who gave it to Thinker.

Thinker lay in one corner of the room, a great shapeless blob of protoplasm. Within him were all the memories of his space-going ancestors. He considered the
picture, compared it rapidly with others stored in his
cells, and said, "No galactic planets within reach."

Talker automatically translated for everyone. It was
what they had feared.

Eye, with Thinker's help, calculated that they were
several hundred light-years off their course, on the galactic periphery.

Every Crew member knew what that meant. Without a
Pusher to boost the Ship to a multiple of the speed of
light, they would never get home. The trip back, without
a Pusher, would take longer than most of their lifetimes.

"What would you suggest?" Talker asked Thinker.

This was too vague a question for the literal-minded
Thinker. He asked to have it rephrased.

"What would be our best line of action," Talker asked,
"to get back to a galactic planet?"

Thinker needed several minutes to go through all the
possibilities stored in his cells. In the meantime, Doctor
had patched the Walls and was asking to be given something to eat.

"In a little while we'll all eat," Talker said, twitching
his tendrils nervously. Even though he was the second
youngest Crew member—only Feeder was younger—the
responsibility was largely on him. This was still an emergency; he had to coordinate information and direct action.

One of the Walls suggested that they get good and
drunk. This unrealistic solution was vetoed at once. It
was typical of the Walls' attitude, however. They were

fine workers and good shipmates, but happy-go-lucky fellows at best. When they returned to their home planets, they would probably blow all their wages on a spree.

"Loss of the Ship's Pusher cripples the Ship for sustained faster-than-light speeds," Thinker began without preamble. "The nearest galactic planet is four hundred and five light-years off."

Talker translated all this instantly along his wave-packet body.

"Two courses of action are open. First, the Ship can proceed to the nearest galactic planet under atomic power from Engine. This will take approximately two hundred years. Engine might still be alive at this time, although no one else will.

"Second, locate a primitive planet in this region, upon which are latent Pushers. Find one and train him. Have him push the Ship back to galactic territory."

Thinker was silent, having given all the possibilities he could find in the memories of his ancestors.

They held a quick vote and decided upon Thinker's second alternative. There was no choice, really. It was the only one which offered them any hope of getting back to their homes.

"All right," Talker said. "Let's eat. I think we all deserve it."

The body of the dead Pusher was shoved into the mouth of Engine, who consumed it at once, breaking down the atoms to energy. Engine was the only member of the Crew who lived on atomic energy.

For the rest, Feeder dashed up and loaded himself from the nearest Accumulator. Then he transformed the food within him into the substances each member ate. His body chemistry changed, altered, adapted, making the different foods for the Crew.

Eye lived entirely on a complex chlorophyl chain. Feeder reproduced this for him, then went over to give Talker his hydrocarbons, and the Walls their chlorine compound. For Doctor he made a facsimile of a silicate fruit that grew on Doctor's native planet.

Finally, feeding was over and the Ship back in order. The Accumulators were stacked in a corner, blissfully sleeping again. Eye was extending his vision as far as he could, shaping his main seeing organ for high-powered telescopic reception. Even in this emergency, Eye couldn't resist making verses. He announced that he was at work on a new narrative poem, called *Peripheral Glow*. No one wanted to hear it, so Eye fed it to Thinker, who stored everything, good or bad, right or wrong.

Engine never slept. Filled to the brim on Pusher, he shoved the Ship along at several times the speed of light.

The Walls were arguing among themselves about who had been the drunkest during their last leave.

Talker decided to make himself comfortable. He released his hold on the Walls and swung in the air, his small round body suspended by his crisscrossed network of filaments.

He thought briefly about Pusher. It was strange. Pusher had been everyone's friend and now he was forgotten. That wasn't because of indifference; it was because the Ship was a unit. The loss of a member was regretted, but the important thing was for the unit to go on.

The Ship raced through the suns of the periphery.

Thinker laid out a search spiral, calculating their odds on finding a Pusher planet at roughly four to one. In a week they found a planet of primitive Walls. Dropping low, they could see the leathery, rectangular fellows basking in the sun, crawling over rocks, stretching themselves thin in order to float in the breeze.

All the Ship's Walls heaved a sigh of nostalgia. It was just like home.

These Walls on the planet hadn't been contacted by a galactic team yet, and were still unaware of their great destiny—to join in the vast Cooperation of the Galaxy.

There were plenty of dead worlds in the spiral, and

worlds too young to bear life. They found a planet of
Talkers. The Talkers had extended their spidery communication lines across half a continent.

Talker looked at them eagerly, through Eye. A wave
of self-pity washed over him. He remembered home, his
family, his friends. He thought of the tree he was going to
buy when he got back.

For a moment, Talker wondered what he was doing
here, part of a Ship in a far corner of the Galaxy.

He shrugged off the mood. They were bound to find
a Pusher planet, if they looked long enough.

At least, he hoped so.

There was a long stretch of arid worlds as the Ship
speeded through the unexplored periphery. Then a
planetful of primeval Engines, swimming in a radioactive ocean.

"This is rich territory," Feeder said to Talker. "Galactic should send a Contact party here."

"They probably will, after we get back," Talker said.

They were good friends, above and beyond the all-en-
veloping friendship of the Crew. It wasn't only because
they were the youngest Crew members, although that had
something to do with it. They both had the same kind
of functions and that made for a certain rapport. Talker
translated languages; Feeder transformed foods. Also,
they looked somewhat alike. Talker was a central core
with radiating filaments; Feeder was a central core with
radiating tentacles.

Talker thought that Feeder was the next most aware
being on the Ship. He was never really able to understand how some of the others carried on the processes of
consciousness.

More suns, more planets. Engine started to overheat.
Usually, Engine was used only for taking off and landing,
and for fine maneuvering in a planetary group. Now he
had been running continuously for weeks, both over and
under the speed of light. The strain was telling on him.

Feeder, with Doctor's help, rigged a cooling system for him. It was crude, but it had to suffice. Feeder rearranged nitrogen, oxygen and hydrogen atoms to make a coolant for the system. Doctor diagnosed a long rest for Engine. He said that the gallant old fellow couldn't stand the strain for more than a week.

The search continued, with the Crew's spirits gradually dropping. They all realized that Pushers were rather rare in the Galaxy, as compared to the fertile Walls and Engines.

The Walls were getting pock-marked from interstellar dust. They complained that they would need a full beauty treatment when they got home. Talker assured them that the company would pay for it.

Even Eye was getting bloodshot from staring into space so continuously.

They dipped over another planet. Its characteristics were flashed to Thinker, who mulled over them.

Closer, and they could make out the forms.

Pushers! Primitive Pushers!

They zoomed back into space to make plans. Feeder produced twenty-three different kinds of intoxicants for a celebration.

The Ship wasn't fit to function for three days.

"Everyone ready now?" Talker asked, a bit fuzzily. He had a hangover that burned all along his nerve ends. What a drunk he had thrown! He had a vague recollection of embracing Engine, and inviting him to share his tree when they got home.

He shuddered at the idea.

The rest of the Crew were pretty shaky, too. The Walls were letting air leak into space; they were just too wobbly to seal their edges properly. Doctor had passed out.

But the worst off was Feeder. Since his system could adapt to any type of fuel except atomic, he had been sampling every batch he made, whether it was an unbalanced iodine, pure oxygen or a supercharged ester. He was really miserable. His tentacles, usually a healthy aqua, were shot through with orange streaks. His system was working furiously, purging itself of everything, and Feeder was suffering the effects of the purge.

The only sober ones were Thinker and Engine. Thinker didn't drink, which was unusual for a spacer, though typical of Thinker, and Engine couldn't.

They listened while Thinker reeled off some astounding facts. From Eye's pictures of the planet's surface, Thinker had detected the presence of metallic construction. He put forth the alarming suggestion that these Pushers had constructed a mechanical civilization.

"That's impossible," three of the Walls said flatly, and most of the Crew were inclined to agree with them. All the metal they had ever seen had been buried in the ground or lying around in worthless oxidized chunks.

"Do you mean that they make things out of metal?" Talker demanded. "Out of just plain dead metal? What could they make?"

"They couldn't make anything," Feeder said positively. "It would break down constantly. I mean metal doesn't *know* when it's weakening."

But it seemed to be true. Eye magnified his pictures, and everyone could see that the Pushers had made vast shelters, vehicles, and other articles from inanimate material.

The reason for this was not readily apparent, but it wasn't a good sign. However, the really hard part was over. The Pusher planet had been found. All that remained was the relatively easy job of convincing a native Pusher.

That shouldn't be too difficult. Talker knew that co-operation was the keystone of the Galaxy, even among primitive peoples.

The Crew decided not to land in a populated region. Of course, there was no reason not to expect a friendly greeting, but it was the job of a Contact Team to get in touch with them as a race. All they wanted was an individual.

Accordingly, they picked out a sparsely populated land-mass, drifting in while that side of the planet was dark.

They were able to locate a solitary Pusher almost at once.

Eye adapted his vision to see in the dark, and they followed the Pusher's movements. He lay down, after a while, beside a small fire. Thinker told them that this was a well-known resting habit of Pushers.

Just before dawn, the Walls opened, and Feeder, Talker and Doctor came out.

Feeder dashed forward and tapped the creature on the shoulder. Talker followed with a communication tendril.

The Pusher opened his seeing organs, blinked them, and made a movement with his eating organ. Then he leaped to his feet and started to run.

The three Crew members were amazed. The Pusher hadn't even waited to find out what the three of them wanted!

Talker extended a filament rapidly, and caught the Pusher, fifty feet away, by a limb. The Pusher fell.

"Treat him gently," Feeder said. "He might be startled by our appearance." He twitched his tendrils at the idea of a Pusher—one of the strangest sights in the Galaxy, with his multiple organs—being startled at someone else's appearance.

Feeder and Doctor scurried to the fallen Pusher, picked him up and carried him back to the Ship.

The Walls sealed again. They released the Pusher and prepared to talk.

As soon as he was free, the Pusher sprang to his limbs and ran at the place where the Walls had sealed. He pounded against them frantically, his eating organ open and vibrating.

"Stop that," the Wall said. He bulged, and the Pusher tumbled to the floor. Instantly, he jumped up and started to run forward.

"Stop him," Talker said. "He might hurt himself."

One of the Accumulators woke up enough to roll into the Pusher's path. The Pusher fell, got up again, and ran on.

Talker had his filaments in the front of the Ship also, and he caught the Pusher in the bow. The Pusher started to tear at his tendrils, and Talker let go hastily.

"Plug him into the communication system!" Feeder shouted. "Maybe we can reason with him!"

Talker advanced a filament toward the Pusher's head, waving it in the universal sign of communication. But the Pusher continued his amazing behavior, jumping out of the way. He had a piece of metal in his hand and he was waving it frantically.

"What do you think he's going to do with that?" Feeder asked. The Pusher started to attack the side of the Ship, pounding at one of the Walls. The Wall stiffened instinctively and the metal snapped.

"Leave him alone," Talker said. "Give him a chance to calm down."

Talker consulted with Thinker, but they couldn't decide what to do about the Pusher. He wouldn't accept communication. Every time Talker extended a filament, the Pusher showed all the signs of violent panic. Temporarily, it was an impasse.

Thinker vetoed the plan of finding another Pusher on the planet. He considered this Pusher's behavior typical; nothing would be gained by approaching another. Also, a planet was supposed to be contacted only by a Contact Team.

If they couldn't communicate with this Pusher, they never would with another on the planet.

"I think I know what the trouble is," Eye said. He

crawled up on an Accumulator. "These Pushers have evolved a mechanical civilization. Consider for a minute how they went about it. They developed the use of their fingers, like Doctor, to shape metal. They utilized their seeing organs, like myself. And probably countless other organs." He paused for effect.

"These Pushers have become unspecialized!"

They argued over it for several hours. The Walls maintained that no intelligent creature could be unspecialized. It was unknown in the Galaxy. But the evidence was before them—The Pusher cities, their vehicles . . . This Pusher, exemplifying the rest, seemed capable of a multitude of things.

He was able to do everything except Push!

Thinker supplied a partial explanation. "This is not a primitive planet. It is relatively old and should have been in the Cooperation thousands of years ago. Since it was not, the Pushers upon it were robbed of their birthright. Their ability, their specialty was to Push, but there was nothing *to* Push. Naturally, they have developed a deviant culture.

"Exactly what this culture is, we can only guess. But on the basis of the evidence, there is reason to believe that these Pushers are—uncooperative."

Thinker had a habit of uttering the most shattering statement in the quietest possible way.

"It is entirely possible," Thinker went on inexorably, "that these Pushers will have nothing to do with us. In which case, our chances are approximately 283 to one against finding another Pusher planet."

"We can't be sure he won't cooperate," Talker said, "until we get him into communication." He found it almost impossible to believe that any intelligent creature would refuse to cooperate willingly.

"But how?" Feeder asked. They decided upon a course of action. Doctor walked slowly up to the Pusher, who backed away from him. In the meantime, Talker extended a filament outside the Ship, around, and in again, behind the Pusher.

The Pusher backed against a Wall—and Talker shoved the filament through the Pusher's head, into the communication socket in the center of his brain.

The Pusher collapsed.

When he came to, Feeder and Doctor had to hold the Pusher's limbs, or he would have ripped out the communication line. Talker exercised his skill in learning the Pusher's language.

It wasn't too hard. All Pusher languages were of the same family, and this was no exception. Talker was able to catch enough surface thoughts to form a pattern.

He tried to communicate with the Pusher.

The Pusher was silent.

"I think he needs food," Feeder said. They remembered that it had been almost two days since they had taken the Pusher on board. Feeder worked up some standard Pusher food and offered it.

"My God! A steak!" the Pusher said.

The Crew cheered along Talker's communication circuits. The Pusher had said his first words!

Talker examined the words and searched his memory. He knew about two hundred Pusher languages and many more simple variations. He found that this Pusher was speaking a cross between two Pusher tongues.

After the Pusher had eaten, he looked around. Talker caught his thoughts and broadcast them to the Crew.

The Pusher had a queer way of looking at the Ship. He saw it as a riot of colors. The walls undulated. In front of him was something resembling a gigantic spider, colored black and green, with his web running all over the Ship and into the heads of all the creatures. He saw Eye as a strange, naked little animal, something between a skinned rabbit and an egg yolk—whatever those things were.

Talker was fascinated by the new perspective the Pusher's mind gave him. He had never seen things that way before. But now that the Pusher was pointing it out, Eye *was* a pretty funny looking creature.

They settled down to communication.

"What in hell *are* you things?" the Pusher asked, much calmer now than he had been during the two days. "Why did you grab me? Have I gone nuts?"

"No," Talker said, "you are not psychotic. We are a galactic trading ship. We were blown off our course by a storm and our Pusher was killed."

"Well, what does that have to do with me?"

"We would like you to join our crew," Talker said, "to be our new Pusher."

The Pusher thought it over after the situation was explained to him. Talker could catch the feeling of conflict in the Pusher's thoughts. He hadn't decided whether to accept this as a real situation or not. Finally, the Pusher decided that he wasn't crazy.

"Look, boys," he said, "I don't know what you are or how this makes sense. I have to get out of here. I'm on a furlough, and if I don't get back soon, the U. S. Army's going to be very interested."

Talker asked the Pusher to give him more information about "army," and he fed it to Thinker.

"These Pushers engage in personal combat," was Thinker's conclusion.

"But *why?*" Talker asked. Sadly he admitted to himself that Thinker might have been right; the Pusher didn't show many signs of willingness to cooperate.

"I'd like to help you lads out," Pusher said, "but I don't know where you get the idea that I could push anything this size. You'd need a whole division of tanks just to budge it."

"Do you approve of these wars?" Talker asked, getting a suggestion from Thinker.

"Nobody likes war—not those who have to do the dying at least."

"Then why do you fight them?"

The Pusher made a gesture with his eating organ, which Eye picked up and sent to Thinker. "It's kill or be killed. You guys know what war is, don't you?"

"We don't have any wars," Talker said.

"You're lucky," the Pusher said bitterly. "We do. Plenty of them."

"Of course," Talker said. He had the full explanation from Thinker now. "Would you like to end them?"

"Of course I would."

"Then come with us. Be our Pusher."

The Pusher stood up and walked up to an Accumulator. He sat down on it and doubled the ends of his upper limbs.

"How the hell can I stop all wars?" the Pusher demanded. "Even if I went to the big shots and told them—"

"You won't have to," Talker said. "All you have to do is come with us. Push us to our base. Galactic will send a Contact Team to your planet. That will end your wars."

"The hell you say," the Pusher replied. "You boys are stranded here, huh? Good enough. No monsters are going to take over Earth."

Bewildered, Talker tried to understand the reasoning. Had he said something wrong? Was it possible that the Pusher didn't understand him?

"I thought you wanted to end wars," Talker said.

"Sure I do. But I don't want anyone *making* us stop. I'm no traitor. I'd rather fight."

"No one will make you stop. You will just stop because there will be no further need for fighting."

"Do you know why we're fighting?"

"It's obvious."

"Yeah? What's your explanation?"

"You Pushers have been separated from the main stream of the Galaxy," Talker explained. "You have your specialty—pushing—but nothing to Push. Accordingly, you have no real jobs. You play with things—metal, inanimate objects—but find no real satisfaction. Robbed of your true vocation, you fight from sheer frustration.

"Once you find your place in the galactic Cooperation —and I assure you that it is an important place—your fighting will stop. Why should you fight, which is an unnatural occupation, when you can Push? Also, your mechanical civilization will end, since there will be no need for it."

The Pusher shook his head in what Talker guessed was a gesture of confusion. "What is this pushing?"

Talker told him as best he could. Since the job was out of his scope, he had only a general idea of what a Pusher did.

"You mean to say that *that* is what every Earthman should be doing?"

"Of course," Talker said. "It is your great specialty."

The Pusher thought about it for several minutes. "I think you want a physicist or a mentalist or something. I could never do anything like that. I'm a junior architect. And besides—well, it's difficult to explain."

But Talker had already caught Pusher's objection. He saw a Pusher female in his thoughts. No, two, three. And he caught a feeling of loneliness, strangeness. The Pusher was filled with doubts. He was afraid.

"When we reach galactic," Talker said, hoping it was the right thing, "you can meet other Pushers. Pusher females, too. All you Pushers look alike, so you should become friends with them. As far as loneliness in the Ship goes—it just doesn't exist. You don't understand the Cooperation yet. No one is lonely in the Cooperation."

The Pusher was still considering the idea of there being other Pushers. Talker couldn't understand why he was so startled at that. The Galaxy was filled with Pushers, Feeders, Talkers, and many other species, endlessly duplicated.

"I can't believe that anybody could end all war," Pusher said. "How do I know you're not lying?"

Talker felt as if he had been struck in the core. Thinker must have been right when he said these Pushers would be uncooperative. Was this going to be the end of Talker's career? Were he and the rest of the Crew going to spend the rest of their lives in space, because of the stupidity of a bunch of Pushers?

Even thinking this, Talker was able to feel sorry for the Pusher. It must be terrible, he thought. Doubting, uncertain, never trusting anyone. If these Pushers didn't find their place in the Galaxy, they would exterminate themselves. Their place in the Cooperation was long overdue.

"What can I do to convince you?" Talker asked.

In despair, he opened all the circuits to the Pusher. He let the Pusher see Engine's good-natured gruffness, the devil-may-care humor of the Walls; he showed him Eye's poetic attempts, and Feeder's cocky good nature. He opened his own mind and showed the Pusher a picture of his home planet, his family, the tree he was planning to buy when he got home.

The pictures told the story of all of them, from different planets, representing different ethics, united by a common bond—the galactic Cooperation.

The Pusher watched it all in silence.

After a while, he shook his head. The thought accompanying the gesture was uncertain, weak—but negative.

Talker told the Walls to open. They did, and the Pusher stared in amazement.

"You may leave," Talker said. "Just remove the communication line and go."

"What will you do?"

"We will look for another Pusher planet."

"Where? Mars? Venus?"

"We don't know. All we can do is hope there is another in this region."

The Pusher looked at the opening, then back at the Crew. He hesitated and his face screwed up in a grimace of indecision.

"All that you showed me was true?"

No answer was necessary.

"All right," the Pusher said suddenly. "I'll go. I'm a damned fool, but I'll go. If this means what you say—it *must* mean what you say!"

Talker saw that the agony of the Pusher's decision had forced him out of contact with reality. He believed that he was in a dream, where decisions are easy and unimportant.

"There's just one little trouble," Pusher said with the lightness of hysteria. "Boys, I'll be damned if I know how to Push. You said something about faster-than-light? I can't even run the mile in an hour."

"Of course you can Push," Talker assured him, hoping he was right. He knew what a Pusher's abilities were; but this one . . .

"Just try it."

"Sure," Pusher agreed. "I'll probably wake up out of this, anyhow."

They sealed the ship for takeoff while Pusher talked to himself.

"Funny," Pusher said. "I thought a camping trip would be a nice way to spend a furlough and all I do is get nightmares!"

Engine boosted the Ship into the air. The Walls were sealed and Eye was guiding them away from the planet.

"We're in open space now," Talker said. Listening to Pusher, he hoped his mind hadn't cracked. "Eye and Thinker will give a direction, I'll transmit it to you, and you Push along it."

"You're crazy," Pusher mumbled. "You must have the wrong planet. I wish you nightmares would go away."

"You're in the Cooperation now," Talker said desperately. "There's the direction. Push!"

The Pusher didn't do anything for a moment. He was slowly emerging from his fantasy, realizing that he wasn't in a dream, after all. He felt the Cooperation. Eye to Thinker, Thinker to Talker, Talker to Pusher, all intercoordinated with Walls, and with each other.

"What is this?" Pusher asked. He felt the oneness of the Ship, the great warmth, the closeness achieved only in the Cooperation.

He Pushed.

Nothing happened.

"Try again," Talker begged.

Pusher searched his mind. He found a deep well of doubt and fear. Staring into it, he saw his own tortured face.

Thinker illuminated it for him.

Pushers had lived with this doubt and fear for centuries. Pushers had fought through fear, killed through doubt.

That was where the Pusher organ was!

Human—specialist—Pusher—he entered fully into the Crew, merged with them, threw mental arms around the shoulders of Thinker and Talker.

Suddenly, the Ship shot forward at eight times the speed of light. It continued to accelerate.

www.ingramcontent.com/pod-product-compliance
Lightning Source LLC
Chambersburg PA
CBHW051925240626
47153CB00004B/1367